The American Game

[A Luther Green Mission]

The American Game

[A Luther Green Mission]

Gary Hardwick

HardBooks Publishing

To Dous,

Gary Hardwick

ISBN Number 9781519543752

HardBooks Publishing
First Edition

Cover Design: Gary Hardwick

Praise For Gary Hardwick

"*The Executioner's Game* is an exciting espionage thriller... grips the audience from start to finish as if a non-stop heavyweight championship between two real contenders is heading to the final round with the loser probably counted out for life."
-Mystery Gazette

That's the landscape for Hardwick's *Darktown Redemption*, this ferocious novel that makes so many other, similar takes on the era read like tame exercises in word spinning. Violence, pain, and anger are palpably real here, and the effect is overpowering.
-Don Crinklaw, Booklist

"*Citycide* is the latest, explosively charged murder mystery featuring gritty, street-smart cop Danny Cavanaugh, a white man who grew up amid Detroit's primarily black underclass. Danny races against time, in this exciting, action-packed saga of murder, mayhem, and brutal struggles for power!
Highly recommended."
John Burroughs - Midwest Book Review

"Far from being a shoot-'em-up, [*The Executioner's Game*] reaches into the psychological and emotional life of the hero, giving insight into the double-timing, dangerous and distrusting world of undercover work."
-QBR

for Uncle Shane,
who loved his brother.

Author's Note

The thrill of getting a call saying a movie studio is going to buy your book is only matched by the disappointment of finding out they are not going to make the movie they loved so much when they bought it.

This was the case when I sold *The Executioner's Game* to Hollywood. I loved Luther Green, my tall, squared-jawed and not to be fucked with hero, the mirror image of Danny Cavanaugh, my urban detective.

Luther is a world-class hero, an assassin who speaks five languages and is skilled in many deadly arts. Also, he just so happens to be Black. So, I was indeed happy when the studio said they wanted to bring him to cinematic life. So, I planned Luther's next mission, the book you are about to read.

But the film did not get made and I was drawn away from Luther and his world, although he makes an uncredited appearance in *Citycide*.

But as fate would have it, Mr. Green and his world of conspiracies and high-staked missions would not leave me alone and so here we are, about to play *The American Game*.

We find Luther older, wiser and even more deadly as he is now trying to find peace.

Thank goodness, he does not.

GCH
July 4, 2016

"America is a nation with a mission— and that mission comes from our most basic beliefs. We have no desire to dominate, no ambitions of empire. Our aim is a democratic peace — a peace founded upon the dignity and rights of every man and woman."

— George W. Bush

"America will never be destroyed from the outside. If we falter and lose our freedoms, it will be because we destroyed ourselves."

— Abraham Lincoln

"Real freedom is heavy; it demands that you become your brother's keeper and accept the painful truth that your quality of life has come from the most evil capacities of men."

— Luther Green

≈≈≈≈≈≈≈≈≈≈≈≈≈≈≈≈≈≈≈≈≈≈≈≈≈≈≈≈≈≈

PART ONE:

THE GLOBAL GAME

"Secrecy is vital to an operation but only
as to your involvement; you want the public
to know what you've done, you just don't
want them to believe that you did it."

- Black Ops Manual

≈≈≈≈≈≈≈≈≈≈≈≈≈≈≈≈≈≈≈≈≈≈≈≈≈≈≈≈≈≈

Prologue

Shadow Of Change

Detroit, Michigan.
September 11, 2001, 3:41AM, EST.

The world was suddenly the smallest place he knew. When he was a kid, he would stand in the wheat fields of his grandfather's farm, looking out on the amber, seeing it meld into the blue sky. The earth was vast back then, a sphere of immeasurable area and infinite possibility.

Now, he could touch every part of the planet, conceive of every hidden corner. Hit a button and send your will half way around the world in the blink of an eye.

That picture played on a loop in his mind, a tiny film with an explosive ending.

Most people led mundane lives, he thought. Only occasionally interrupted by anything interesting and rarely intersecting the incredible, just a man with a job, a family and an inconsequential purpose, dust in the wind.

Things like a car accident, a suicide or a murder were all events you heard about after the fact, making them removed, unreal and unlikely to ever happen to you. Most people were small in the scheme of life and they were just fine with it.

But something was coming and not only was it that rare occurrence, it was going to galvanize all of those small people and change them forever. We would be thrust into a deadly world but unable to do a damned thing about it.

And it was not so much what was going to happen that made his mind whirl, but the reasons behind it, the sheer force of imagination that had brought it into being.

He was not particularly patriotic but this was something that he felt some pride about. He was, in his own way, going to be part of history. His name would never be in a book or his face on TV, but there would be some, a few, who would know his part in this story.

*How many times throughout history had men like him
served the cause of justice, recruited to a higher purpose and
performed anonymously? With all the wars and revolutions
of man, there had to be an army of faceless soldiers who had
altered the course of mankind and would never get any
credit.*

*He had been handsomely paid for his service, though. The
thick envelope in his jacket reminded him of that. Even in
theoretical causes, realities had to be met and money was
always a way of settling those accounts.*

*He stopped at a traffic light on Woodward and Davison.
The night was winding down and the street people were out.
Two young black men in hoodies stood on a corner smoking.*

*A homeless man pushed a cart on the other side of the
street, its shaky wheels rattling. He looked to be in a hurry.*

*"This fucking city is a shit-pile," he said to himself. He
barely remembered when this was a nice, decent place. That
was like a dream someone had stolen and the memories
taunted him sometimes.*

*As a kid, he'd spent a lot of time at this corner, taking the
bus from here to either side of town. The Southeast corner
had a Burger King on it, one of the first in the city, and he
could remember many a meal there. There was a bank on the
other side of the street back then. He couldn't remember the
name of it. And the Chicago-Davison bus ran down the
service drive across Woodward into the waiting arms of
Detroit's east side.*

*He turned onto that service drive and headed east. From
somewhere in his mind, he recalled that this stretch of
freeway was the very first in the nation.*

*Detroit and cars. Cars and Detroit. The city would be a
thousand years old and that connection would never change.*

*Suddenly, he saw a dark SUV in his rearview. It looked
like a GMC, triple black, dark windows, standard
government issue. His hands tightened on the steering wheel
as he realized the SUV was pacing him, or so he thought.*

*There wasn't a lot of traffic this time of night and hadn't
he seen a similar vehicle before?*

He felt for the gun he was carrying, took it out of his jacket and placed it on the seat next to him.

The SUV accelerated and switched lanes. He grabbed the gun in his right hand and got ready. He'd only have one shot if it came to that.

He eased up on the trigger as the SUV over took him and then turned a corner. Suddenly, he realized that he was only traveling about 30 miles per hour, slow even for the service drive.

He could not be too careful. Disposing of five bodies in one night was a very tricky undertaking. It had not been the plan to have so many, but the last target had gone home and so all the people there were forfeit. Rules of the game.

When his last task had gone from one dead to three, he had recalculated his burden with the casual ease of changing a dinner reservation.

This was the last plant of the night. He'd picked out all the other spots early on, but was forced to improvise when the body count had changed.

Again, his mind drifted to the past. How many people had been killed to arrange the murder of JFK in Texas or Lincoln in Washington? How many bodies might still be buried under freeway lanes and buildings? Something like that took elaborate planning and for any life-altering event, part of the price was always calculated in blood.

He drove past the connection to I-75 and went to the end of the freeway into the adjoining neighborhood. This was a dead-end place, filled with ruined homes and lives. It was perfect for his endeavors. Life was cheap here and people knew how to keep their mouths shut.

He wondered if the city would ever come back from the abyss it had fallen into. It couldn't go much lower, he thought. They'd pretty much hit bottom, so there was no way to go but up, really.

Cities died long before they knew they were dead, he mused. Their insides turning to dust and dirt and the decay of humanity shattering its ambitions like so much glass in a gunfight.

He hooked a left turn and drove down a street that had no sign posted on it. He knew this street, he thought distantly.

It was dark and all the streetlights were broken, save a couple at the end of the corner and their light was very dim.

"Yep, rock bottom," he thought and stopped midway down the street. He got out of his car, taking the gun with him.

The air was crisp and there was a faint smell of burned wood and cloth on it. Something had been on fire recently, probably a house or maybe a car, he thought, catching a whiff of a metallic odor.

Something skittered quickly across the street from him, low to the ground. He gripped the gun and his eyes zeroed in on an old wrecked car.

A thin, sickly looking dog ran from behind the car and turned up the street and away from him. At least he thought it was a dog. It moved pretty damned fast for a canine. He waited until it was gone and then released the weapon.

"The fuck was that?" He whispered to himself.

He sighed a little, then opened his trunk and dragged the last body out. It was heavy dead weight. Why did dead bodies feel heavier than live ones?

The corpse was wrapped in thick plastic and lime had been layered in three rolls. He put a harder plastic on the outside and tied it into a rope-net with some thick old carpet on the underside at one end. This made it quiet and easier to drag. It looked like a long, fat roll of fabric. On one end, there was a small bag with two cans inside.

He grabbed a shovel and took the body behind an abandoned house. He stopped in the backyard of the dilapidated home, which tilted uneasily upon its foundation.

Something rustled in the thick weeds in the back of the yard. Rats, he thought or whatever that dog-thing was.

He looked up to the sky and the night was clear, a beautiful sight compared to where he was. But the night would not last for much longer, so he had to get going.

He took off his jacket and dug a shallow grave. The ground was hard and each shovelful unearthed debris, garbage and wormy soil.

These people never cleaned their yards, he thought, just let weeds and dirt cover their living waste like a goddamned anthropological dig.

He had a quick thought of uncovering a dinosaur bone. More than likely, he'd find a body already buried here. But he did not. And after a moment, he was lifting rich looking soil from the ground and piling it up nicely a few inches from the open hole.

He was wet with sweat when he finished the job, his shirt clinging to his chest and sides. He rolled the body into the hole. He took the small bag that was attached to one end of the body and pulled out the two cans of coffee inside. He opened them and poured the coffee on the body. He dropped the cans inside and then quickly filled in the grave.

A dog with a keen sense of smell might catch a whiff of the dead body even through all of its wrappings but the coffee would throw them off.

"No chances," he said to himself.

He put his jacket back on, absently feeling for the money, which was still there. He moved out of the backyard and could sense the morning coming. He needed to get back home so he could watch the events unfold. He didn't know an exact time, but he was not planning to go to sleep for a while.

Some of the bodies might be found, but when the morning came, no one would be thinking about murders in the local cities. In the morning, the heavens would be sounding red alarms and death would be viewed in global measures.

He went back to his car, opened the trunk and placed the shovel inside. He'd have to ditch the ride, maybe leave it for the locals to strip. But that was too risky, he thought. No, he'd take it out and set it on fire. No need to help the authorities if by some miracle they put this all together.

His last thought on earth was not to forget to break the shovel and throw it away in sections.

The gunshot sounded like a muffled pop, like someone had uncorked a bottle with a bass voice.

The man was hit in the head and fell onto the lid of the open trunk. He twitched for a second, his body trying to right itself as the bullet disrupted all the communications inside his brain.

A dark stain appeared on his pant leg as his bladder emptied itself. He coughed loudly and slumped forward, his body arching slightly then stopping as the trunk lid caught his weight.

Another figure walked up quickly to the dying man. He pushed his body into the trunk, turning it, so that he fell head first inside.

The killer removed the dead man's car keys, the envelope and the gun and then shot him again in the heart and one last time in the head. He then tossed the shovel inside.

The killer closed the trunk, got into the car and drove out into the coming day, followed closely by the black GMC.

1

Turks

Kavala, Greece

Luther Green was perfectly still as he sat on a girder above the men. He was clad in an old E-1 stealth suit, lightweight material with a Kevlar II chest plate. It looked black but was actually a very dark blue. And there was no more E-1, he corrected himself. The secret department of assassins which worked under the CIA and the Department of Defense had been disbanded and it was all his fault.

It had been quick. He and presumably all the rest of Elite One had gotten a message which sent them all to other agencies. All activities had been shut down while someone erased the unit from memory.

Luther was still part of the CIA but he suspected that he also worked for the State Department and the DOD. He wasn't sure where his orders were coming from but it didn't matter who signed his paycheck, the job was still the same: eliminating America's enemies with prejudice.

In a way, this was actually better. Not having any ties to anything official meant he was free from all of that chain of command shit which had led their last Director to wake up one day thinking he was God.

Luther carried a Baretta CX-4 Storm and a Sig Sauer shotgun which was strapped to his back and his trusty Walther P99, comfortably in a leg holster.

He was in the best shape of his life. He'd lost weight and gained muscle in the last year. He remembered the doctor telling him that his body fat was a mere 2%.

When he thought in percentages like this, he was in combat mode. This was good because it had been a long time since he was sent on a non-recourse, multiple kill mission, essentially an execution.

It always seemed foolish to send one man to eliminate several until you thought about it. You may be out numbered, but a single man had no team to worry about and one of the first things he learned at E-1 was you are more likely to be killed by the mistakes of others than yourself.

Firepower could also tip the scales for a single assassin and then there was the biggest advantage, surprise.

In the old E-1 days, he'd have a TWA, a tech and weapons advisor. This was a Man Friday who was smart and kept eyes and ears on everything. Now, there were these faceless voices who watched on satellites and you didn't know where the hell they were.

Luther's old TWA, Marcellus Hampton was now a big shot in the Pentagon's Cyber Unit. He was fighting a war in another dimension.

Luther looked forward to missions with something akin to glee. It sounded sick but after being in the business for so long, he'd learned that he was just like any other man with one difference, he knew the truth about himself and humanity.

Every society needed its killers, alpha men and women who kept society balanced and civilization safe. He was no different from the car salesman who loved tricking you into buying accessories you didn't need. Hell, even God had a team of assassins, he called them Angels.

Luther was in an old machine parts warehouse in Kavala, Greece. The Vakalis Brothers had supplied parts for heavy trucks and earth-movers for over thirty years, but their business had gone under in the crash.

Ironically, there were no Greeks below him. These men were from Turkey with one American according to his intel. They were freelance suppliers for terrorist groups, including the one called ISIS, the newest scumbags on the anti-freedom list.

This is why he'd gotten the kill order. Apparently, we hated these guys and didn't want to leave any doubt about it to them or the world.

Luther had left Detroit after the fall of E-1 and settled in D.C. He hated the capitol place with its fat cat lobbyists, cowardly politicians and predatory women.

He lived in a very nice condo where high-clearance government types resided and had been trying to get out more and date, something that he detested. It was so hard to meet women, even though they seemed to like him just fine.

Modern women were very aggressive and for those in their fertile years, that urge to bond and settle a man down was a fierce prime directive, one that Luther avoided at all costs.

Once his family knew he was still alive, he had re-bonded with them only to leave again. This was not a popular decision, especially for his mother who had visions of weddings and grandchildren.

She could not fathom that Luther would ever do any of the things his job entailed. His father knew though, and his silence on the subject told Luther he had an ally.

But he did find a nice girl in Detroit, an FBI agent. It had been good for a while. Good times, laughs and great sex. But it had ended badly when she wanted him to be stationed in the U.S. and give up international travel. Well, the sex was not *that* great and he moved on.

After he relocated to D.C., Luther had come home one day to find Neal Land, a friend from the CIA waiting in the lobby. Neal was a homey from Michigan, a smallish man with a rather big head from Grand Rapids, who always smiled.

Ordinarily, Luther didn't trust anyone who smiled so much but Neal was one of the exceptions. Man was just happy most of the time.

They exchanged pleasantries and then Neal left, after giving Luther a packet with his next assignment.

Luther opened the envelope with dread. His last mission had been to kill his friend, Alex Deavers, a legendary agent in E-1. It had ended not in a kill but the collapse of E-1 itself.

Luther had found evidence linking the U.S. to the invention of what became HIV and a plan to subjugate Africa with it. He presented this information to the President in exchange for him helping the African nations. Yes, he blackmailed the President, a neat little notion that Luther liked to think of as *bluemail*, patriotic persuasion.

The President kept his word and there were now at least three experimental vaccines for AIDS and one very good preventative pill.

But when the President left office, business as usual came back and now Africa was being divided up by other world powers and fucking Ebola was back. Luther didn't know what to make of that but it did not feel good.

The new President needed the Middle East wars calmed and that was good for Luther because when overt wars ended, the covert ones, amped up.

America was on a mission to destabilize the Middle East, while the economic powers that be were moving forward to new measures.

Money and war were always good business for an assassin.

Luther had recorded kills in three different countries and had been party to as many neutralizations of terrorist sympathizers, men and women who did not understand the depth of their complicity in global politics but who nonetheless had to die.

The Vakalis Building was relatively small as warehouses went. It was constructed of a rather cheap wood frame and had probably gone up quickly. It had an elaborate steel frame inside that was used to haul the heavy machine parts from one side to the other and load into crates or onto trucks for moving. This made for a perfect assassin's perch.

There were no immediate neighbors. The area was once a thriving industrial town, but the last banking collapse had doomed it along with all the little businesses that had sprouted up in support.

Terrorists loved dead cities and towns and Luther didn't think it was just the isolation that attracted them. They also loved to live where capitalism had failed, where dreams and freedom had failed.

Luther had been living in the basement of the place for two days, watching the men, while their comfort level rose.

The cellar was another quickie job, a big hole really with one way in and out until Luther made a tunnel which led to the outside where he relieved himself into containment bags, an embarrassing but necessary action. When the mission was over, he would burn them with a standard accelerant.

The men he targeted had no official name. They were shipping money, medicine and weapons across the sea to Turkey. From there, who knew where the contraband was going.

This was not a big operation but one of their shipments had found its way into a bomb that had killed five Marines. So these men were being used to make a bigger, more important statement.

Luther was told to wait for the kill order and then execute as efficiently as possible. This had become difficult when he saw the men bring in a young girl and assault her on his first day there.

He kept telling himself that if he moved to save her, many others would die as a result. So he didn't act but he did make himself watch, loading his anger into storage for later.

Two of the men took turns on the girl. The first man did it in full view of the others. Only two of the men watched this. The second man at least had the decency to assault the girl in a back room.

Luther burned with rage and had almost thrown the mission away but he would make sure that someone intercepted the girl before she could be sold again.

The girl was shipped out the next day with a crate filled with ammunition and several crates of medical supplies.

There were nine men below him, all killers probably and it was his mission to take them out before the locals got there.

Luther's support team would wait the standard time and then call the police so that it would make the news and America's enemies would know we were on the job and not to be fucked with.

A drone strike was considered at one point but there were men in the government who considered drones a coward's way out of a fight. The collateral damage they had caused in Iraq had been terrible, ultimately embarrassing and worse, costly.

Luther personally hated the idea of drones. Killing should be done by men, so that no one ever forgot the heavy price it carried. If the humanity were ever taken out of war, we were all doomed, he thought.

The three men below him would have to be dispatched quietly. The other six were all in a room entertaining themselves. They would resist but that's what the firepower was for.

"You are a go," said a voice in his ear. *"Repeat, you are a go."*

Luther moved into position. He grabbed the side of another steel beam, shifting his weigh to his arms. His legs jutted out before him, while his hands held the steel beams that hung from the ceiling. His arms were locked, suspending his entire body in a sitting position, gymnast called an L-hold.

Luther took in a deep breath, then released himself from his perch and fell on the man in the middle of the three, while pulling his battle knife.

Luther landed on the neck and shoulders of that man, driving him face first into the ground and crushing his upper spine. He could hear it make a dull crunch as he landed.

Luther quickly delivered a punch to the throat of the man to his right. The man grabbed at his throat and gagged.

Luther spun, dropped to his knee and severed the other man's femoral artery on his right leg. As he rose, Luther brought the knife into his liver, then lung and finished with a slash to his throat.

Luther pivoted gracefully and plunged the blade into the eye of the man he had punched who was recovering and pulling his gun. The man fell to one knee. Luther removed the knife, spun around him while cutting his jugular.

All of this took about seven seconds.

Three down.

As Luther surveyed the kill, he saw the man he had fallen upon move. He was not dead yet. But that's not what alarmed Luther. The man was holding a pressure alarm and his hand was releasing it. When he let go, it would signal the other men in all likelihood. If Luther was really unlucky, it would detonate something nearby.

He did not have enough time to grab the alarm and so Luther pulled the Baretta Storm and ran toward the room in the back of the place.

The idiots had put themselves in a room with no windows and only one door. The men had become so comfortable, that they had left only three men to guard, while they played cards and watched porn. Luther

knew this because he'd set up a camera in that back
room and had them on a head's up display.

Luther moved swiftly as the alarm went off. On his
head's up feed, he saw the men charging to the door
with weapons. He saw three AR-15's, two Uzis and—

"Fuck," said Luther as he saw what had to be a
sniper's rifle.

That guy had to go first, Luther thought as the door
flung open. The sniper's rifle had high powered
rounds. One shot and you were done.

The men with the AR's began to shoot. Luther
pushed them back with a burst from the Storm, settling
in behind some wooden boxes containing some of their
contraband.

Inside the room, Luther saw the sniper setting up on
a table. He was going to let the AR guys distract Luther
and then try to get a shot.

Luther pulled a mini gun stand and snapped it open.
He set the Storm up on it and put a firing clip on the
trigger and set it to semi auto. He would let it fire in
bursts while he moved away. When the mag was
empty, the AR men would fire again and he'd have his
chance at the sniper.

The men yelled at Luther in Farsi. He knew what
they were saying but he did not answer. No need to fall
for that trick and give away his position.

Luther let the Storm fire as he moved to his left. He
settled behind more wooden crates. All the while, he
was counting shots. The mag was almost empty.

Luther pulled the P99. It was tricky from this
distance but he had to try.

Suddenly, the Storm dry clicked and shut off
automatically.

The door to the room flew open and the AR men
fired at where Luther used to be.

When the door was open, Luther saw the sniper in
the rear on a table laid flat with his gun pointed out the
door. Luther fired the P99 once and saw the man's head

pitch to one side as he fell off the table and onto the floor.

Four down.

The AR guys were startled by the shot and Luther caught them in the head with three shots from the P99.

Seven gone now. Two left.

Luther quickly jumped up, put the P99 away and swung the Sig shotgun up.

As the final two men came out, Luther cut them down. The first, he shot in the thigh. He crumpled in front of the man behind him who tripped over his body. As they fell, Luther caught the second man in the chest. He fell backwards, his Uzi pistol flying into the air.

The first man he'd shot with the Sig managed to get off a burst at Luther but it missed. Luther pumped the Sig and fired again shattering the man's hand. The man yelled as he feebly tried to stop the blood.

Luther put the Sig away and took the P99 back out and silenced the last man with a shot to the head.

"*Meeting over,*" said Luther into his com as he fired safety shots into the heads of the fallen men.

"*Acknowledged,*" said his contact. "*Base wants the American's body returned.*"

"Acknowledged," said Luther.

Luther had known for a while which one he was. He was the one with the pressure alarm on him.

Luther went back to that man. Now that he was done, he noticed that another big shipment was in the place. Two assault vehicles sat in the middle of the room along with a cash of guns and bomb detonators.

Luther collected the American's body, put it on a dolly and dragged it behind him as he left the place. He stopped just briefly to set fire to his containment bags.

As he moved off, he heard the police and others coming up a road. When they got there, they would find the carnage and the dead, evidence of America's authority.

The foreign press would try to cover up the story, to say it was a rival criminal organization or some other such contrivance, but America's friends would counter with stories of terrorism and retribution by local sympathizers to Western democracy.

In the deluge in facts and information, the governments of our enemies would know that the United States had taken out another cell.

This would make our enemies very nervous about their activities and they would in all likelihood slow down or even cancel operations in some cases.

Luther's SUV was a quarter mile or so away, hidden in another abandoned building. He quickly made the trek to it.

Luther loaded the body inside, turned on his music, a hard-biting tune by Kendrick Lemar and drove off to meet his contact.

2

Curse

Paris, France

Luther stood as the debriefing team entered *La Miche Trois* in Paris. France's core of special agents, *Les Aigles* were small in number and were mostly used for intelligence work these days.

They originated from the Resistance during WWII and were known for their rigorous training. Now m they worked within The General Directorate for External Security, France's equivalent to MI6 or the CIA.

Most agencies debriefed with as little fanfare as possible. In Germany, it was done electronically. In France, they still preferred things the old-fashioned way, face to face.

Cari Leaux was *Les Aigles'* third in command. Formally, the communications officer, she had deep political ties. In fact, her family could boast having at least one high-ranking member in France's government for the last hundred years.

Cari was a tall woman at six feet but her legs were longer than they should have been even for a woman of her stature, perhaps two inches but enough that she seemed like a freak of nature, like God wanted you to notice those legs.

She had a keen mind and had specialized in advanced scenarios during training. Cari was a regular on international terrorist think tanks, trying to keep a step ahead of their actions.

Cari was also Luther's former lover. Their history was not all good and it had ended rather badly and so Luther had some dread about this meeting.

"Good morning, agent," said Cari.

"Cari," said Luther casually, countering her formal tone.

He was not going to act like there wasn't history here. Everyone knew the now famous tale of how he had saved her from a terrorist cell and had killed her then boyfriend who was a double agent.

The love affair had gone on for over a year, until Cari's family forced the issue of their future. Cari stood up to her parents, one of whom was very high up in the State Department.

But it was Luther who had ended the relationship, confessing that he was not looking for a committed future. Cari had not taken it well.

She had tried to kill him.

Or at least that's the way the story was told. The facts are that she dispatched Luther as sniper backup for an extraction team in Yemen but his placement had been discovered and he was almost killed by a counter sniper. Luckily, the other man was sloppy and Luther caught sight of him just before the other sniper pulled the trigger.

Cari had conveniently forgotten to tell him of the chance of another sniper, or so the tale went. The truth was Cari didn't know of the other sniper but that did not make for a romantic tale for the French.

"Greek locals are reporting the incident as in-fighting," said Cari, "but the network is already saying the West is making incursions into the euro cell structure."

"Isn't that true?" asked Luther.

"Not for you to know," said Cari.

Luther saw one of the other two men suppress a smile.

"I have a few questions about your initial report," Cari continued. "Some things we have to make sure are consistent before our people answer questions. The President is speaking at a terrorism summit in three days and we want him to be able to offer that France took part in this."

"Fine," said Luther. "Shoot."

Cari asked him several innocuous questions and Luther could not tell if she was toying with him or being thorough. And to make matters worse, she looked great. Her skirt hugged her hips, giving just hints of the toned body underneath and she could never find blouses that could hide her generous upper endowment.

Cari also had the most beautiful hands, an unusual thing for a man to notice. Luther remembered that she had been a hand model when she was in college. He couldn't stop himself from igniting memories of what she had done with those perfect hands and soon, all of their amorous adventures came back in a flood.

"I think that covers it," said Cari. "You should remain here in case there are further questions, normal incubation time."

This meant that he should wait to see how the world would handle the killings. If they bought the official story, then he'd be free in a few days, if not, then there would be a decision as to whether he had to go into hiding while they cleaned it up.

That almost never happened as the public was quick to consume any and all acts of violence as the price of whatever conflict story they were being fed.

Also, during normal incubation time, the information crew run by Cari would be out in force doing disinformation and counter-disinformation to further confuse the public.

This even included conspiracy theories about the hit that would be technically accurate but in the hands of the most non-credible sources.

At the agency, you were taught that the truth was like acid, it would burn through anything and so people didn't really want it. They liked their truth filtered, buffered, diluted and much of the time, they didn't want it at all, just whatever version of it made them feel comfortable on the sofa watching reality shows.

Cari and her people left Luther in the debriefing room. She was being unusually cold for some reason and he was curious about it. Beautiful women had big egos and he knew he had bruised hers. He made a mental note to at least speak with her about being cordial and professional.

He retired to the agents' lounge which was a local bar where government types hung out. In France, there was not a hierarchy like in the U.S. A paper pusher might drink and eat with a senior agent. No one wore the badge of their profession, only that they served mother France.

Luther saw a familiar face and headed toward him. Michel Besson was a man with a very lusty personality. Luther didn't know exactly what he did but he suspected Michel was a technical expert for the state. He had been secondary backup on a couple of assignments. Michel carried a weapon which mean he was certified but mostly he was always carrying transmission equipment and decryption devices.

Luther greeted him in French.

"English, please," said Michel. "I am working on mine. Your French is lovely but I need practice."

"Why?" asked Luther as Michel poured him a glass of wine.

"I am headed to your country soon, New York. I will be traveling with our Ministry of Commerce."

"Good for you," said Luther. "I bet that's a nice assignment."

"Yes," said Michel. "You go, monitor and fuck your very eager women."

Luther would bet the women were eager for Michel. He was a very handsome man who looked like the old actor Paul Newman, with his steel blue eyes and sandy hair.

"I'm in no hurry to go back," said Luther.

"Rumor is, there is going to be a shakeup in your country's international representatives," said Michel.

Luther could scarcely think of anything more boring than matters like this.

"Don't care much for such things," said Luther.

"You never know, one of them may need to be eliminated."

Luther was mildly shocked. Michel had never indicated that he knew or suspected what Luther did until now. Perhaps he was just making a joke, Luther thought, but Michel was not laughing.

"What's the shakeup about?" asked Luther, not wanting to respond to the last statement.

"Trade pacts, currency exchanges and other such banalities. It seems that your west coast is thriving from the trade agreement but their reciprocal partners are not sharing."

"I'll have to look into it," said Luther. Suddenly, he wanted out of this conversation. Michel was drinking a lot and he had broken social protocol by talking business.

But before Luther could think of an excuse, Michel had invited two ladies over who looked like they were still in high school. They were in their early 20's and completely giddy as the handsome Frenchman made small talk and jokes.

The girl designated for Luther was pretty and very friendly but Luther wanted no part of a sexual tryst. This was not a problem an hour later, when Luther made an excuse to go. Michel was happy to entertain both ladies on his own.

Luther made his way back to his quarters in a local hotel. Paris was always particularly beautiful at night. He should have been thinking about Michel in a three way, but he was still wondering why Cari had been so strange in their brief meeting.

He admitted that he was still a little stuck on her. They had indeed been compatible but Luther was not ready to give up the life for any woman, no matter how perfect she was. The agency was still his love.

His eyes widened a little as he stepped inside the lobby of the hotel. Cari was at the end of the lobby bar, which faced the front door.

She had two drinks in front of her, which meant some man had approached her and tried to pick her up. She had also changed clothes, which meant that she had come with a purpose.

As Luther checked out her evening ensemble, he knew what that purpose was. Her hair was up and she was wearing a short red skirt with a stark white blouse and jacket.

He approached her but did not say anything. She glanced at him, not making eye contact for more than a second. Then she downed her drink and walked out.

They went to his room and she immediately began to disrobe for him, slowly deliberately, still not looking him in the eyes.

Naked, she walked to his bed and lay face down.

This was one of the fantasies he had imparted to her when they were together. A stranger clad in red let herself be picked up from a bar. No names were exchanged. She would come to his room, get naked and lay down for him to take her from behind. No words, just the act.

Luther was also naked before he finished remembering it all. His clothes were scattered with hers, tangled on the floor.

As she heard him approach, Cari raised up on all fours, extending herself. Luther moved in behind her, feeling her warm skin. He stroked her back and she spread her knees further, accommodating him. He savored for just a second, then he entered her.

She uttered loudly and slammed her ass into him as hard as she could. And then he heard her laugh, a low sweet sound that filled him with even more energy.

She undid her hair and it fell about her shoulders. Luther grabbed it and pulled as he thrust forward. This was also part of the fantasy.

He wanted to see her, turn her around and finish between her legs but that was not the deal. He quickened his pace and Cari responded in kind. They each caught the rhythm and soon they were one in their desire and motion.

He came, pulling her to him as hard as he could. She arched her back up and he could feel her shudder and pulse around him.

They had always had such good chemistry, he thought. Cari had always claimed she could time her orgasms and he never doubted her.

Luther broke the connection and Cari stayed in position for a moment, bent over, legs apart. Luther looked at her there, unmoving like a memory. This was also part of the fantasy. She would not move until he touched her again.

Luther placed his hands on the small of her back and Cari lowered herself down and rolled over. He was pleased to see the most satisfied smile on her face under the cascade of her hair.

Luther lay next to her but did not move in. He waited for her. This was not part of the fantasy but something that they had grown accustomed to.

Cari lifted a hand to his face and pulled him to her and they kissed and as always she gave him two kisses at the end, one on the lips and one on his left cheek. He had never asked why she did that but he knew it meant that she had not forgotten him.

"So?" She said after some time.

"Exceptional," said Luther.

"Everything you wanted?" asked Cari in a rather melodious tone.

"And more."

She laughed again and he was beginning to feel concerned. The contrast from the two meetings couldn't be more different. He decided to tell her the truth, a dangerous thing with a woman but she deserved it.

"I have been missing you," said Luther.

"That's comforting, Luther, but I cannot say the same. I've been very busy and haven't had a lot of time to think about you or us. But when I saw you, well, here I am."

"Coulda fooled me," said Luther. Cari never lied or pulled her punches. "I thought maybe I was slated for termination."

"Not a chance," said Cari and then she laughed again. "People are afraid of you after the Deavers thing. You know, you're the only men to ever both win the Executioner's Game."

"So people keep telling me."

"Where is Alex again?"

"I don't know," said Luther. "He could be anywhere. You know him."

When one E-1 agent is assigned to terminate another, the mission is called the Executioner's Game internally. Usually, only one agent emerges and the legend is, if the rogue agent (the wolf) killed the pursuer, the agency would leave him alone. That was a nice thought but in E-1's history no wolf had ever survived— except his friend Alex Deavers.

"I did not try to kill you, you know," said Cari. "But I think it makes me very exotic for people to think so."

"That's one word for it," said Luther. "So, what does this mean, Cari? You want to start up again?"

"No. In fact, I'm engaged."

Luther felt a small pang in his gut. He remembered that Cari was always a surprising mate and while this kept things exciting, it also came with bombs like this.

"So you're using me? I would have enjoyed it more if I had known that." Women, he thought. They were the most lethal weapons on the planet.

"I am not going to marry the fool," said Cari. "But the engagement keeps my family at bay. They are pressuring me like you would not believe. My mother had my doctor do a fertilization projection chart on me. She knows the exact number of days until I can no longer have children."

Cari had a younger sister who was also single and no brothers. The family name was going to die if the girls didn't get to reproduction soon.

"I am on the pill by the way. So, don't worry."

"*Confiance*," said Luther. This was a short hand code they used. They both came from a world where almost no one could be trusted. They had vowed to never deceive each other in romance. He knew she would never trap him that way.

"I'm so sorry about that," said Luther.

"But not sorry to hear that I am not in love, yes?"

"Yes," said Luther not wanting to hide his feelings anymore. He waited a moment, then said: "I would not make a good husband, Cari."

"I know," she said somberly. "But you would be good at all the rest of it. That's better than most women get. Take my father. He is a liar, a cheat, a coward and a bastard. He likes girls to piss on him, can you believe that?"

Luther believed it all and he did not ask how she knew. Cari was a fine agent and she had obviously checked up on her parents.

"But he's been a good father to you, hasn't he?"

"*La meilleure*," said Cari. "I have the most wonderful memories of him. He cried when I lost a spelling bee and bought me the biggest ice cream I'd ever seen. We both got sick."

"I'll slow down one day," Luther said.

"But you'll be old and you'll marry some twenty-year-old and keep her happy with Viagra."

Luther couldn't imagine a more dismal life. In truth, he didn't know what came after field work. He imagined that he might die on a mission and never have to face getting old.

"Life is so much better when you don't have to think about it," Luther said softly. "I never wanted to hurt you."

"But you did. Such is life, yes?"

"*Oui.*"

It was these times that gave him amnesia. He could see nothing wrong with her, with them, as a couple. Everything was good at this moment, while he was sated by sex and her sweet laughter. But tomorrow, the light would bring back all of their flaws and his apprehension. He savored the moment, this time of perfection, but as with all things good; it was fleeting.

"*Et il en va,*" said Cari.

The phrase was one she used often. It was a term used by the writer Kurt Vonnegut, a cue that another life has passed, or is passing in his works. To Cari, it meant another moment in time is gone.

"And so it goes," Luther repeated in English.

Cari got up and went into the shower. Luther waited a moment and then joined her.

Luther slept alone that night. He and Cari made love in the shower and then she'd gone back home. She did not believe in sleeping over when the relationship was not solid. She had a point. Those sun-drenched goodbyes were the worst when you knew you may never see the person again.

Luther got up and ordered breakfast. He munched on toast as he searched for Cari's fiancé online. He found him quickly as the announcement had made the news.

Bernard Tache was the son of a millionaire and an actress. He was a handsome devil and that made

Luther a little jealous. They made a striking couple and
suddenly, he found himself wanting to forget her, this
attractive nuisance to his heart.

Luther went into *La Miche Trois* early and checked in
with his American contacts. He was congratulated on
the mission and told that the cover and disinformation
was working fine. He was ordered to take a vacation
and wait for his next assignment.

The girl who had been assaulted by the Turks was
alive and returned to her family. That made him smile
a little. There was some justice left in the world, he
thought. And the American turned terrorist was sent
back to his people and already the U.S. was pushing a
radicalization story that showed the pitfalls of turning
against democracy.

When he was done, Luther went into a secure area
and placed another call via computer. It took some time
as what he was doing was not technically legal or
authorized. After their various security measures were
defeated, he was on the line with Alex Deavers.

"How are things?" asked Luther.

"That you in Greece?"

"Yes. Sloppy."

"Very," Deavers laughed. What was your weapons
compliment?

"Sig shotgun, Baretta Storm and my sidearm," said
Luther. "Missing the action?"

"Some," said Alex. "Some game we play, huh?"

"I'm not sure who the players are anymore," said
Luther. "I am certain that these ISIS people are partly a
creation of our aggressive fuck ups but what do they
want? They cannot win."

"That's what they said about Saddam but he ruled
for decades. So, I'm living in Las Vegas now," said
Alex.

"With all those cameras?"

"No one looks for old spooks in Sin City. Besides, my face has healed and I look different now. I'm living with this exotic dancer. She's nice. Likes to play."

"I bet. You know, if you came in—"

"They'd rendition me. No, I'm happy where I am. I do a little work now and then, fixing things for people."

"Don't make too much noise," said Luther. "You know there's a military installation out there."

"I know. God knows what kind of shit they do," said Alex.

"One of the agents here said things are hot back home. Any idea what it is?"

"People are being turned up for some reason. The media is fostering divisiveness more than usual and the violence is off the charts. Chicago is like a shooting gallery."

"Domestic? Why would we be trying to rile up people domestically?"

"I don't know," said Alex. "Sometimes, that's the best way to get the people behind you internationally, get them mad at each other and then say we're all Americans against some foreign nation."

"Another war?" asked Luther more to himself. "No way we can handle another one."

"When you come back, come to Vegas, I'll have my girl save you a lap dance."

"I'll hold you to that."

"How's your family back in Detroit?"

"Okay. I made the deal."

After his mission with Alex, Luther had made a deal with the agency to protect his family as an asset of the state. He no longer had to worry about them being put into play on any of his missions. The only people he had to worry about now was the agency itself and he guessed that was the best he would ever do.

"Sorry I tried to kill them," said Alex.

"Given what was on the line, I would have done the same thing."

"Hey, didn't you have a serious girl in Paris?"

"I did or I do," said Luther. "It's hard to tell these days."

"Well, keep your head low," said Alex. "Women have a way of getting you to do things."

"Might be too late for that," Luther confessed.

"Keep safe," said Alex.

"You too," said Luther.

He ended the call and settled back at his digs. He wanted to get out of Paris but had to remain close. He knew just the place.

3

Killsurance

Aix En Provence, France.

Luther strolled the cobblestone street and hurried to avoid one of the many tourist busses that traveled the streets of *Aix En Provence.*

The bus rolled by and could see the faces of the tourists, their cell phone cameras waiving around, trying to get some footage of the beautiful town.

He'd decided to put some distance between himself and Cari. Seeing her fiancé had nothing to do with it, he told himself but that was a lie. He was trying not to become a further complication in her life. He'd already slept with her, that was bad enough.

The little town was a picture perfect place, a city-commune in the south of France, about 30 clicks north of Marseille. It looked like a kid's fairytale, with its collection of monuments from the Roman Empire; Cistercian monasteries and hilltop villages.

Under this grandeur, it was just a college town with several universities within its limits and lots of young, pretty boys and girls. It was also the location of one of America's safehouses.

Aix was a laid back town and the people, the *Aquisextains* as they were called, were very friendly. It also gave him a chance to speak exclusively in French, which he loved to do.

Luther moved into a business area and wondered when he would find peace in his personal life. He certainly didn't think he'd ever be a suburbanite husband with loud kids and a rusty barbecue pit but there had to be some kind of end game, even for a killer of men.

Luther stopped at *Pâtisserie Béchard* and bought some dark chocolate for later. France had spoiled him for cheese, bread, wine and chocolate. The French prided themselves on all four products and didn't allow GMO's and the tampering that the West did.

Luther ordered his chocolate in perfect French and was pleased when the clerk did not give him the slightest bit of surprise.

"*Merci*," he said and he left the shop.

As soon as he stepped outside, Luther was sure he was being followed. It had been just a passing thought at first, but now he was certain of it.

He marked the movement and images behind him. He even kept track of things in his peripheral sight. After a while, a pattern emerged, which usually meant someone was following.

It was not an enemy or they would have struck by now or perhaps they were waiting for an isolated spot. With this in mind, he did not head back to his safehouse. No need to give the tail that information.

Luther didn't glance back as he headed for a fashion area where there would be lots of people and reflective surfaces. He was there for just five minutes, when he caught a glimpse of his tail.

Luther smiled a little, then pretended to get a call and headed toward his tail. She tried to turn off but it was too late. He'd spotted her just as she was about to turn into a shop.

Sharon Bane had a smile on her face but her eyes said that she was upset that she'd been caught. The angular blond woman moved toward Luther and embraced him in front of a cafe.

"Damn you," said Bane.

"Hello to you too," said Luther.

Sharon Bane was one of Luther's former colleagues at E-1. She was a top agent and had an impressive list of successful missions.

When Luther turned rogue agent, she and a group of others were sent to kill him. He had shot her with a tranq dart in Detroit, knocking her unconscious. He didn't feel bad about it; she had shot him with a bullet.

Bane stood just under six feet and had a lithe, athletic body. She had large blue eyes and a mane of blond hair that she almost always wore in a ponytail.

Today, she wore a pair of leggings that showed off her figure, a t-shirt, a jean jacket and a Royals baseball cap. She looked like a tourist.

"You were always lousy at tailing, Bane," said Luther.

"I knew I was dead when you headed for all of these storefronts. When did you know?"

"Why are you tailing me is the better question," Luther countered.

"Heard you were in France and I know you hate Paris."

"You know I don't hate Paris.

"And how is she of the long legs?"

"Good," Luther said. "Engaged in fact."

"Wow. Are you okay?" asked Bane with genuine concern.

"It was a shock but I'm good. I hope it works out, he said."

"That's a lie," said Bane. "Let's sit. I'm thirsty."

They went to one of the many little cafes and took an outside table and ordered drinks. Men passed by and turned to get a look at Bane who was stunning when not in disguise.

All agents knew how to change and alter their appearance to blend in. It was a simple matter of moving closer to one of the Basic Looks they learned in training. For Luther, it usually involved facial hair, baggy clothes and a jawline change. For Sharon Bane it was harder. She had to make herself less attractive and that was difficult.

"I was reassigned to London after the fall," said Bane. "Not a lot of action there but I visit other areas close by."

Ukraine, Luther thought. A Ukrainian rebel was targeted by the Russians. The Russian assassin had himself been killed right after he came into town disguised as a businessman. The hit had been clean. It looked like a terrible car accident. That had been Bane's hit.

"Well, I'm flattered that you came all this way to say hello to an old friend," said Luther knowingly.

"You're so damned cynical," said Bane as their drinks arrived.

"So what's the story?" asked Luther.

"Still seeing that agent, the American?" asked Bane still not ready to talk. There could be many reasons for this, thought Luther but the first one that occurred to him was that her reason had danger attached to it.

"No, it's off," said Luther.

"You don't seem like the kind to ever settle down," said Bane.

"Look who's talking. You got more exes than I can count," said Luther.

"A girl needs her recreation."

Bane was known to have a rather voracious sexual appetite and liked one-nighters. She and Luther were only friends but he did have the occasional thought. It was always followed by the adage about shitting where you eat.

An awkward silence crept up between them. Luther liked Bane but she didn't fly from London to France for a latte. Now he wanted her to get on to it.

"Some people were working the intel backend of your last mission. We were trying to find out who was bankrolling the terrorist suppliers in the region."

"I assumed it was the usual scumbags," said Luther. "And what did they find?"

"We have been experimenting with a new facial scan technology. We're set up in major airports back home and with Interpol here."

"Right," said Luther. "Heathrow was one of the first to get it, I recall."

"We got a lot of false hits and a few scores, took in some Syrians looking to start trouble but nothing big. Then one day, we got a seventy percent hit on a file on the U.S. classified list.

"An undercover?" asked Luther.

"Yes, but the man in question was dead," said Bane. "MI5 put a tail on him and the CIA was called."

"Why was he in the data files, if he's dead?" asked Luther.

"The system uses all the data we have," said Bane. "I can only guess that it uses all faces in case one of us is impersonated. This guy, the dead guy, was not impersonated."

"So, how did it get to you? Or should I ask why?"

"Because of the name that came up. It was one of our people. Let me show you something," said Bane. She pulled out a mini tablet and turned on a video.

Luther strained a little to see it in the sunlight, so she handed it to him. The video showed a man walking out of a shop in London. He was medium height and unspectacular looking.

"I took over and followed the suspect. I took this video after seeing him at a play," said Bane. "He's let his training lapse because he never caught on."

Suddenly, Luther saw it as the man turned, he saw the lines at his jaw and neck indicating cosmetic surgery.

"He's been fixed," said Luther. "A good job too."

"Watch his walk," said Bane.

Luther did and the man had a gait with a slight limp on his right side. He was trying to hide it, probably with a higher right shoe but it was there. And then the man stopped at a vendor on the street and bought a drink. He paid the man and then saluted him with three fingers, like a boyscout.

"Meyerson?" said Luther. "It can't be."

"That's what I thought," said Bane. "I don't know anyone else who has that particular gesture. He'd be fifty-seven or so by now."

Peter Meyerson was what they called a Server, a collector of classified information from multiple agencies. He was one of those guys you'd see standing with the President's staff one day, with the Secretary of Defense the next day and then on the ground in a war zone a week later.

The government loved Servers because they all had perfect memory, never kept records, were battle tested and could be easily eliminated if need be.

Meyerson was one of the best. Phi Beta at Princeton, Navy pilot and graduate of the CIA's Prisoner Resistance Program, a set of tests where students learn to resist extreme torture and interrogation techniques.

Luther had taken the PRP and would never forget the pain associated with it. Meyerson had legendarily passed without so much as a wince.

Meyerson was the only Server assigned to E-1, a job that had lasted for ten years. Whenever Meyerson was around, you knew the hit was coming from on high and was urgent. And when he left, he always saluted with those three fingers.

Luther had done three Meyerson jobs, including one that had almost cost him his life in Brazil.

"Pete Meyerson died in the 9/11 attacks," said Luther.

"Easy enough to fake your death that way," said Bane. "He was in the building, we know that. Question is, how did he get out?"

"Easiest way would have been as a first responder," said Luther casually.

"Watch the second video," said Bane. "It took me a lot of surfing the web to find it."

Luther watched another video. It was the day of the world Trade Center attack. A local news service was doing a report. That day came back to him suddenly. He was in North Africa on a mission that'd been called off after the attack.

Suddenly, a fireman walked by in the background of the video. Luther paused the video and saw a man that looked like a fireman. He was wearing a mask over his face. He was totally legit— except for the watch he wore, a Rolex Daytona with gold accents.

"That could be him," said Luther. "So, you told your handlers about your suspicions."

"And they told me to verify and then take him out," said Bane.

Luther was surprised. Meyerson was a valuable asset but there hadn't been incidents, intel lapses, which could be traced back to him. If he had just disappeared to escape his life in America, why would the CIA want him dead? Why not reacquire him, debrief and then decide?

"I get it," said Luther. "Makes you wonder why Meyerson wanted out."

"Just like when they told you to kill Deavers. It smells."

"Where is Meyerson?"

"Not sure yet. But I'm on it."

"You want my help on this?" asked Luther. "Do our people know?"

"I told them I may have to recruit. They know I'd go to you. Why wouldn't I?"

Luther was mildly flattered. He was sort of famous after the mission that ended E-1 and facing down a President.

"Meyerson is a tough hit if he hasn't gone soft and he probably has countermeasures wherever he's living,"

Luther was already going into mission mode. He was definitely intrigued by this situation and its implication to their new masters.

"I wanted to pick your brain about why we'd want him hit," said Bane.

"The most obvious reason," said Luther, "is because you found him in the first place. Maybe Meyerson was supposed to disappear and he broke the deal."

"Interesting," said Bane. "Never thought of that one."

"Why didn't you take him out in London? And what the fuck was he doing there in the first place?"

"I wasn't sure he was Meyerson then," said Bane. "It took time to get a confirm and by then, he was gone. I had a tracker on him so I'll know where he went soon. And the other question was answered when I checked the actors in the play. One of them was Chet Meyerson, his son."

"You think his family knows?" asked Luther.

"No. His wife remarried and even adopted a kid. I think he's been keeping tabs on them on the web and wanted to see his son."

Luther's eyes suddenly brightened. He was way ahead of Bane who saw this and smiled a little.

"You want him alive, don't you?" asked Luther.

"Yes, because there's one more thing. I am being followed but I shook my tail this morning."

"Jesus," said Luther. "Insurance?" In his head, he thought *killsurance,* which is what agents called it. The agency never liked to take chances and often a backup agent was sent to insure that a mission was fulfilled.

"Yes. If I fail, he completes the mission and probably he kills me when it's over."

"Then that's our first mission," said Luther. "I take him down."

"Nothing fancy," said Bane. "We'll knock him out and house him for a few days."

"You do realize what we're doing if the agency sent him?"

"Yes," said Bane, "but after what happened in Detroit, how can we ever say it's not right?"

Luther was already thinking of the many different nonlethal ways to take down a fellow agent. He had hoped to have a few days of rest but it seemed he was once again about to become a rogue agent.

4

Oddjobs

Luther waited on the rooftop as the wind stirred up
again. He'd been waiting patiently since the sun set.
The roof of the office building had a gravel floor,
perfect to hear an intruder's approach. There were big
vents and air conditioners all over.

Luther picked one about halfway between the ledge
facing Bane's building across the way. If he were
watching Bane, this is where he'd do it.

After he and Bane had made their pact, he'd gone
back to his place and gotten together all the equipment
he'd need, a tranq gun and his P99, fitted with a
silencer.

The agency had finally solved the gun silencer
problem. Most silencers were only good for one or two
shots and then, the gun barked as loudly as it normally
would. The agency's new silencer was actually a sonic
transfer device that converted the sound of the shot
into energy, which was stored in an ion battery
chamber which itself powered the silencer.

He also carried a high-powered tranq gun filled with
the agency's newest knockout potion.

Luther's plan was simple. He'd watch the man, see
what kind of surveillance was going on and then hit
him with the dart. From there, he and Bane would
interrogate him and then send him back home.

Once uncovered, the agency would call off whatever
the hell this was and trust Bane with her mission.

Forty minutes later, Luther heard the door to the
rooftop open. A figure walked out, clad in dark clothes
and carrying a bag. It was a man, about thirty or so
with dark hair. His skin was olive and he had a finely
edged beard. Middle eastern, Luther thought vaguely.

The man walked to the ledge and Luther took this opportunity to get into a shooting position while the man crunched gravel beneath his feet.

The man didn't check the area, Luther thought. He'd probably been coming here for several days and had gotten comfortable.

The man set up by a big vent and took out a gun and quickly assembled it.

Luther's pulse quickened. This man was here to kill Bane, he thought. The weapon looked to be a Blaser, R93 Tactical but the scope was different by the look of it.

Luther removed the silenced P99. He could hit this guy easily from this distance, he thought.

After snapping on the gun sight, the hitman, pulled a cell phone and waited. Luther eased his hand on the P99 and waited.

A tense moment passed as Luther could tell the hitter was waiting on a kill order. What the fuck had Bane gotten him into?

The hitter's cell buzzed. He checked it and then suddenly unsnapped the gunsight. He quickly took apart the Blaser and put it back into his bag. He then removed a black box, pressed a button and put an earpiece into his ear.

He was listening to Bane's room, Luther surmised.

"More bullshit," said the hitter in Hebrew with an accent that was Israeli. He settled in, removing a thermos and raising the sight to his eye. "Maybe I'll get to see that lovely ass again."

Luther pulled the tranq gun when he heard the door to the roof move. The hitter sprang up and raced to the door.

Two men came through the door and the hitter caught them off guard. He struck the first man in the throat and kicked the second before he could do anything. The hitter finished off the first man with a blow to the temple.

The second man threw a blow but the hitter caught the punch, tripped the man to the ground and dropped a knee into his chest. He finished him with two blows.

The hitter rifled through their clothing and pulled out two pouches of white powder and a thick envelope.

"Fuckin' drug dealers," said the hitter with contempt. He tossed the powder down a pipe and pocketed the envelope, which probably contained money.

The man had exceptional skills, Luther thought. He was definitely a pro, probably Mosaad. And he had not killed the two men when could have easily done so.

While the hitter had dispatched the two men, Luther had moved from his position to behind the fight. Luther had the tranq gun raised and ready.

Suddenly, Luther saw the hitter go stiff for a second and he knew the man had sensed him. The hitter reached into his coat and turned just as Luther fired the tranq dart. The dart hit the hitter in the side of the neck.

The knife he'd thrown sailed at Luther who easily dodged it.

"Fuck..." said the hitter as his eyes rolled and he fell to one knee fighting the drug. "...me."

****

Luther and Bane sat playing cards while they waited for their captive to come to. They were playing Texas Hold 'Em and Bane was killing him. She was a really good player and Luther suspected she counted cards, a skill that he'd never been able to master.

The hitter had no identification on him of course, not even a hotel room key, which could have led them back to his hideout.

Luther and Bane ran his prints and his face through digital recognition and had gotten nothing yet. Luther figured whoever he worked for had done a good job of protecting his identity, or more likely, he was a burned agent.

The hitter's phone was a cheap disposable and had no numbers in it. He probably got a new one each day. The call he'd gotten had come from a blocked number.

They secured him to a steel chair Bane had borrowed from her hotel. They took his weapon from him.

The envelope the hitter had taken off the drug dealer contained ten thousand euros. Luther kept that as well.

"You can stop playing possum," said Bane sensing the man was alert. "The dart should have worn off a guy as big as you ten minutes ago. He's probably been sitting there, looking for weaknesses, thinking he'll get a chance to get us. He's trying to work those plastic ties we put on him. That's what I'd be doing."

"My only regret," said the hitter, coming out of his act, "is I didn't get to see you undress again."

"Aggressive tactic," said Bane. "Trying to see if I'll be pissed off about him seeing me naked. Or to see if you react. He's thinking you're my man and if you get jealous, then he'll know that much more. I'd be more concerned why I'm not dead if I were him."

"Am I supposed to be afraid because you said that?" asked the hitter. "Well, I'm not."

"Still trying to get information," said Bane. "Persistent but not too bright. If it was me tied to a steel chair, I would wonder what they were going to do to me to get information. Maybe beat me or shock the chair. That would be very painful."

"You dodged my knife," said the hitter to Luther ignoring Bane. "Where did you learn that trick? He doesn't talk? You Americans with your good cop bad cop. I watch TV. This doesn't work."

Luther had been silent all through their exchange. He had barely looked at the hitter. Now he looked to Bane who nodded.

Luther took a gun from the table they played on. It was a small caliber weapon and it had a sonic silencer on it.

The hitter laughed. "What? Am I supposed to be afraid of—"

Luther shot him.

****

The hitter flew backwards and tipped over in the chair. He hit his head on the floor as he yelled in pain.

The bulletproof jacket they had put on him stopped the bullet but not the impact of the shell in a tiny area.

The hitter yelled as he felt a jolt of pain near his shoulder where he'd been shot. The blonde woman sat him back up. These two were crazy, he thought.

"Now that we understand each other," said the woman, "you know if you don't talk, we'll kill you."

"You fucking *shot me!*" said the hitter. He was angry and starting to sweat. No doubt these two were pros and he was in trouble.

The black man sat at the table counting the money he'd taken. He was playing the bad cop but he seemed ready to dispose of the hitter if he had to. In fact, while he played possum, the hitter had heard the black man suggest this to the woman but she had demurred.

The hitter's eyes narrowed. He locked on the woman, trying to see if there was any room for him to negotiate. She did not even blink and then he slumped in the chair ever so slightly.

"Who are you?" asked the black man.

"So, he does talk," said the hitter.

"We checked the database and there's no record of you," the black man continued. "You obviously have training but you are not one of us."

"Not enough training," said the woman. "And you were not sent by my agency. So, who are you and please think about your answer."

Defeat passed in the hitter's eyes. He reacted particularly to the word *agency*. He realized he'd been sent after a pro. He knew he had to make the first move.

"Sason Zoabi," said the hitter.

"Who hired you?" asked the woman.

"My agent gave me the contract," said Sason. "He or she is not a known commodity."

"Give us a name," said the black man

"I don't have one," said Sason, wincing again. "I get a dossier and half payment, the other half when I am done."

"What was your mission on her?" asked the black man. "And if you say you don't know, well, I wouldn't if I were you."

"To follow and watch," said Sason. "And if told, to eliminate."

"When is your checkpoint?" asked the woman.

"I don't know," said Sason. "How long have I been out?"

"An hour," said the black man.

"You're going to check in as you always do," said the woman. "Then you're going to tell us everything."

"Nothing to tell," said Sason. "I never get any information. May as well let me go. Also, give me back the money I took from those drug dealers. It's mine."

Suddenly, the woman laughed. And it was tinged with evil. Ironically, she never looked more beautiful to Sason who had been watching her for days now.

"Is this some kind of sick game?" yelled Sason. "What the fuck is so funny?"

The black man raised the gun and shot him again.

****

"We can do this all night," said Luther. "Maybe the next one will be outside the jacket."

Sason was covered in sweat now and was clearly breaking.

"Sick fucks, both of you," said Sason.

Luther turned to him with the gun and leaned in.

"You're in the game like us, you know how it goes down. You want to have loyalty to some asshole who wants you to kill another pro, fine. You'll die in this hotel and no one will ever remember how noble you were."

Sason blinked some sweat from his eyes and heaved a long breath. "My agent is Guy Damaseaux, he doesn't know I found out who he is. After my second job for him, I had to know. He lives in Belgium."

Bane went to her computer and opened a secure line to her home base. She typed in the name.

"Got several hits," said Bane. "It's an alias but we'll narrow it down."

"So, did you drop out of Mosaad or are they looking for you?" asked Luther.

"Looking," said Sason. "I failed to execute on a mission and well, you know how that is. They burned me. Right now, I don't exist."

"Why?" asked Luther.

"I took out the bad guys, a husband and wife team in Damascus. They had two kids. They were supposed to be asleep but they saw me... my protocol says they all have to go, but I couldn't."

"And they want you killed for that?" asked Bane.

"You were in The *Shah Khohr*," said Luther.

"There is no Black," said Sason and he smiled a little.

Just like the CIA has E-1, so did every intelligence agency have a band of secret killers. The Russians had The *Svellveats* or Column, the Chinese *Dāopiàn* and The Germans the aptly named *Reuger Klasse*. And the Israelis' Mosaad had *Shah Khohr* or The Black.

"When you live surrounded by a hostile enemy, there is no room for weakness," said Sason, his eyes looked far away for a second. "I should have killed them, for my people."

Luther had never stopped watching Sason. Even when a subject was distressed, deception recognition techniques worked. Everything he knew told him Sason was being truthful.

"We're going to cut you loose," said Luther. "If you try anything well, you can only kill one of us, the other will kill you."

"E-1," said Sason.

"There is no E-1," said Bane and then she took a small cutter and broke the ties that held him.

"I will need to check with my agent," said Sason. "Otherwise, he will know I have failed."

"You can do that on the way."

"What?" said Sason.

"You're coming with us to get him," said Luther.

"I just love road trips," said Bane.

Sason looked at the two of them, slight smiles on their faces, looking forward to mayhem. He sighed.

"Crazy fucking Americans."

5

Wallon

Phillipeville, Belgium

Kastell Ravi flipped the button and the bomb pack exploded.

It lifted a column of water a good twenty feet into the air. The water shot straight up and then expanded and fell like an isolated rain. It dotted the lake's face and sounded like a very loud sizzling as it cut through the quiet. Just as quickly, it was gone and the man-made lake absorbed the disturbance like a parent does the outburst of a child.

Good, he thought, very good.

Ravi was on a remote part of the *Eau d'Heure* lakes in Belgium just outside of Phillipeville. The locals would think it was kids fooling around again or maybe the government who sometimes allowed *Armée belge;* to perform exercises.

Every year, Ravi came here to detonate part of a set of explosives he kept under his shoppe in the city. He had about twenty kilos of a nifty little explosive he got on the black market. The stuff was reliable but became unstable after a time and so he had to make sure it was still good. It was.

Ravi did not sell the explosive. It was in his shoppe in case his real occupation was ever discovered. He would press the brown button under the front counter, and the entire block would just vanish in fire and sound.

Only once had a component failed to explode in the lake, only proving that he had to constantly replace them.

He walked back to his car and made his way back to the N-40 and was soon back in Philippeville, where he was Guy Damaseaux, a nice Walloon merchant and a widower.

He'd gotten into the agenting business after his stint in the French military. He was French by birth. His father was a French mutt and his mother Walloon and Iranian of all things. It was a strange mix that served him well because Ravi had always looked rather Italian.

He was still handsome at sixty, even though he had a bit of a paunch and was balding on top. He could still get the attention of a lady if he played his hand well and he always did.

Ravi was ousted from the service and fell in with some other military reprobates who became mercenaries for hire in the modern era of endless wars. He was mainly an organizer and procurer of goods and he was good at it. Those were good times. Raids, kill parties and lots of money and sex.

When the gang got older, Ravi trafficked in the many killers for hire he'd known over the years. He set up a system which protected his new identity and then he just raked in the fees. It was not exciting but it was a good life.

Ravi walked right by Luther as he opened his shoppe right on time that day.

"He's in," said Luther into his cell to Bane who was nearby.

Ravi got the usual parade of tourists and the same locals. When no one was looking, he'd check his secure phone to see how his people were doing.

Ravi perked up a little when a dark-haired woman entered the shoppe. She was shapely and wore sunglasses. She looked American to his trained eye but he was a little surprised when she spoke in German which was not unusual in a country with three national languages.

She ordered a sweet blend of loose *tabac* and paid for it.

"Are you on holiday?" asked Ravi smiling. He never missed a chance to flirt with a pretty tourist. Many of them were very adventurous, especially the American ones.

The shoppe was empty and he briefly fantasized about something happening between them.

"*Nein*," said Bane. "I am here to meet someone actually, a man named Ravi."

Ravi stiffened at the sound of his real name. He did not panic because Ravi was not an uncommon name. Still, he moved to the right toward the detonator. So many times, he felt the button and thought of the day he'd have to use it. It was cold on his fingers as Bane matched his movement.

"You are free to wait for him," said Ravi.

"*Danke*," said Bane and moved to a shelf to look at some exotics.

Ravi eased a little. It had been nothing. Ravi watched Bane for a second more, admiring her legs. He took care of another customer and then the place was empty again except for Bane.

He could make his move, he thought. Maybe she'd like a quick one in the back. He caught her eye and she smiled.

"*Nice place sie hier, Ravi,*" said Luther from behind Ravi.

Ravi turned around and saw Luther. How had he gotten inside? He moved back to the button and now he felt his hand apply gentle pressure on the detonator.

Still, he was not sure what danger this was. He worked for many concerns and sometimes, they checked on him. These two did not look like government types and the black man spoke in German as well.

Ravi stiffened when the dark-haired women removed her wig and Ravi remembered her. She was a mark. He just could not remember her name.

"Who are you people?" asked Ravi.

Bane went to the entrance and put the "closed" sign up.

Ravi said a little prayer and pressed the button. But the heat and the light did not come. Instead, Luther walked to him and held up two thick blue cables.

"We've been here all day, Ravi," said Luther. "Of course, we knew you'd have some kind of escape plan. Imagine our surprise, when we found the ultimate one."

Then a third man entered. It was Sason who looked at Ravi with anger.

"It is customary to tell a man when he is on the case of another pro," said Sason.

Ravi bolted for the back of the place but Luther caught his arm and twisted it out, holding him.

Ravi yelled in pain from the hold.

"We need to know who paid you to hire this man," said Luther. "I am only going to ask once because I am sure the answer is here somewhere. We don't want to waste time looking for it but if you give me any grief, I'll break this arm and then we'll get it anyway."

"Mustavo," said Ravi but it is probably an alias. "I have all of his contact info on file. My system is in the column in my office."

Bane left and returned with a Signet-A5 satellite computer. Luther released Ravi.

"I want my full payment," said Sason.

"Why? You did not complete the mission," said Ravi.

Sason snapped a kick into Ravi's face so fast, that Luther did not have time to pull the man away. Ravi's head snapped back and he fell unconscious.

"You could have waited until after I got the password," said Luther.

"Sorry," said Sason.

"There's cash in the office," said Bane.

Luther revived Ravi after a few minutes. Sason raided the office and came back smiling and holding a big stack of bills which he put in one of Ravi's store bags.

"I am taking all of this," said Sason, "for all the trouble you've caused."

Luther said nothing but he was putting together the story on the former Mosaad agent. The money was needed for living and staying hidden but Luther suspected Sason had family somewhere he was sending it to. Family made an agent vulnerable. No one knew this better that he did.

Ravi gave Bane the password and soon she was smiling.

"He used the old tactics and codes but I think I know where he is," she said.

"You are going to go out of business Ravi," said Luther. "Whatever your plan B was, you should get to it."

"I will," said Ravi. "I will retire, yes and go away."

It happened very quick. Sason moved to Ravi and stabbed him through the heart. When he let him drop to the ground, there was a letter opener buried to the hilt in Ravi's chest.

"What the fuck!" yelled Bane.

Luther said nothing. He knew Ravi had to die. It was just not his job to do it. Ravi knew killers, many of whom probably owed him favors. He was too dangerous a man to live.

"I had to," said Sason. "I will cover this. You two should go." Sason was already running from Mosaad and The Black; he could not afford to let Ravi live.

"Burn the place," said Luther, "and take all the valuables and dump them where they can be found. That'll throw the police when people sell them."

"We are going," said Bane. "Give us an hour, then do it quickly."

6

Run

Evora, Portugal.

Luther and Bane flew out of Belgium on the private plane of one of America's many wealthy contacts. In this case, it was a family named Veiter who were big in oil and hotels officially but connected to many other sketchier enterprises.

Luther eased in the comfort of his chair on the G-650, the plush leather squeaked a little beneath one bare arm. The ice in his cranberry juice clinked quietly as the plane banked shortly after the takeoff.

He disliked private planes. They made him painfully aware that his life was in someone else's hands. On a commercial airliner, he felt like just another passenger in the hands of fate.

Something else was troubling him and he could no longer deny it. It was that agent's feeling, that instinct when your deeper capacities have worked something out beneath your conscious mind. He didn't know exactly what it was but something was rotten on this mission.

How does the government lose an asset like Meyerson and then randomly pick him up? He thought.

It's hard to disappear from the government's radar. Then again, after 9-11, the world was in chaos and resources were poured into the two wars.

To most people, the Iraq and Afghan wars seemed like folly but only if you didn't understand America or global politics.

Our goal, which was probably hatched decades before, was to destabilize the region and break the Islamic monarchies and dictatorships.

We didn't care what the religion was, as long as there were democratic governments and capitalist economies involved and if we had to attack the religion to accomplish this, then so be it.

Maybe Meyerson wasn't down with the war plan and cut out so he wouldn't have to be part of it. Many Pentagon higher ups were demoted in the wake of the two wars and not one media outlet reported on it. Suddenly, Luther was as eager as Bane to talk with Meyerson.

"I hate it when I see you thinking like this," said Bane taking a seat opposite him. She held a drink.

She was wearing an all black outfit that left little to the imagination. The bottom looked like yoga pants and he could almost see through them. Her hair was down and she had on light make up.

Bane was a purposeful woman and well aware of her sexuality. He wondered why she had picked this outfit.

"Just putting some facts together," said Luther.

"Me, too. I'm wondering why Meyerson ran and why we never caught on."

"Meyerson is smart," said Luther. "He may have been planning an escape for a long time."

"We can't count on that," she said looking a little concerned. "There may be something bigger involved."

They were going to Portugal just outside of a little city called Evora. Their intel told them that Meyerson was there in a compound under an alias. They did not have a lot of time before Meyerson found out Ravi was gone and then he'd disappear.

"If he's still a good agent, he has at least two safehouses in case of emergency and an escape plan," said Luther.

"Meyerson's living under the name Bernard Davidson," said Bane, "a businessman who has retired to his grandparents' homeland and so he could have safe houses anywhere without them drawing too much attention."

"Why are you dressed like that?" asked Luther abruptly. It was good to work with Bane but she did shit like this that drove him crazy.

"Pilot," she said flatly. "He flew me a year ago. I flirted and got nothing. That's not gonna happen again."

"Just give it to him," said Luther smiling a little.

"I just want him to try," said Bane. "I'm not sure if I'm still interested."

Luther's smiled faded a little as he thought again of Cari. He would never understand women.

Bane took out her iPad and on a map, Luther saw Meyerson's compound sat in the middle of several acres of land. It was flatlands that had been cleared decades ago. Now thanks to wealthy investors, it was a lush, serene meadow.

"Meyerson's nearest neighbor is about a mile away," said Bane. "He has a mobile security team supplied by a company called S.A. Francisco, who polices the entire area.

"We could try to knock off a security team but it's problematic," said Luther. "If we're discovered, it severely shortens our escape time."

"We could pose as government types," said Bane. "We have contacts in Portugal."

"I'd bet Meyerson has someone on his payroll already. I would. So if we do that, we have to be careful."

Luther took the iPad and expanded the map's view.

"Okay, we assume he has safehouses but how does he get to them in the event of an attack?" asked Luther. "There's got to be a secret way out. And if it can be used to get out…"

"I'm on it," said Bane.

She went to her computer and began to type. She pulled up lists of major construction jobs in the last

twenty years. It didn't take long for her to find that
Meyerson commissioned a big job five years ago. The
specs on it had been destroyed but the government had
a copy.

"Meyerson commissioned a home addition. What he
really built was a tunnel," said Bane. "It goes out of a
basement and surfaces a half klick from the house."

"Good," said Luther. "Let's get a precise location
and we're on."

Bane got to work laying out the rest of their mission
expertly. Luther was impressed as she meticulously
made the action plan.

By the time they landed, Bane had their mission
completely outlined, including a contingency plan and
escape alternatives.

As Luther deplaned the G-650, he saw the pilot hand
Bane a card. Her personal mission was accomplished
too, he thought.

They moved into the city quickly. Luther called
ahead and had their local contacts get them into a
cleaning company that had access to the homes near
Meyerson's.

The owner of the company was under indictment.
He had been running narcotics and had gotten caught
in a sting. He was a valuable asset because he had
access to so many of the wealthy people in the area. His
smuggling van would come in handy as well. That's
where Luther and Bane would hide on the trip.

"So, you scored with the pilot?" Luther asked as
they drove to the cleaning company.

"Of course," said Bane. "I might fuck him. He'll be in
Rome in a week."

Bane had a victorious smile on her face and Luther
knew in that moment that she would never sleep with
the pilot. It was all about her ego and she had won.

They arrived at Lagos Cleaning and went inside the
business entrance. Their contact, a middle-aged agent
named Pauman guided them through.

From there, Pauman took them into the transportation building where they got into the bottom of the truck's floorboard. It was a tight fit and they were literally on top of one another.

"Try to keep your hands to yourself," joked Bane.

"No promises," said Luther.

Once they were hidden, the cleaning crew was brought in and were none the wiser. Only Pauman who was the driver, knew the truck's real cargo.

When they arrived at the house next to Meyerson's, Luther and Bane waited until the cleaners were gone. Pauman opened the compartment and released them.

"Everything looks good," said Pauman. "Good luck, my friends."

Luther and Bane moved to the rear of the house by the garage. It was a clear shot to Meyerson's house which he could see in the distance.

They took off running. They sprinted hard, headed for a small mound between the homes. Luther felt good as he got pumped up and Bane kept pace with him, her athleticism showing.

They stopped after a few minutes, both breathing harder. They had a map, which Bane had on her cell phone. They searched the area for the opening.

"Don't see it," said Bane. "According to our map, it should be here."

Luther saw groups of bushes nearby. There was one mound that was bigger than the rest. It looked very green and lush compared the other surroundings. Luther ran over to it and felt a leaf. It was plastic.

"Got something," said Luther.

Bane ran over to join him. She smiled as she felt the fake foliage and saw a vehicle.

"There's a jeep in these bushes," said Luther. "The entrance has to be close."

Luther and Bane began to circle in opposite directions, moving out from the jeep.

"Got it," said Bane. She stood over a patchy growth covering a manhole.

They lifted the manhole cover and entered, climbing down an iron ladder which looked relatively new.

"He hasn't had this tunnel for long," said Luther. "Hopefully, it won't have any enhancements we need to worry about."

"Damn, we're gonna have to carry his ass up this thing on the way back," said Bane. "Assuming we don't get killed."

They got to the bottom and saw a long dark tunnel that had to be a dead run to the mansion. There were a few lights before them but they seemed to fade after a while as Luther looked down the passage.

Repetition is one of the many keys to a successful mission. Luther and Bane had gone over it many times already but they did so again as a matter of common practice.

"Our intel is that Meyerson's at home entertaining," said Luther. "He's not married but has a girlfriend who lives with him. All told, there are ten or twelve people at the compound, not including security."

"There are five guards stationed at the house," said Bane. "The forward men won't see us coming. We're only concerned with the two in the rear and the one who patrols the home itself."

With that, they moved toward the house. The floor of the tunnel was moist and pitted with holes. Meyerson had not made any refinements.

Luther ran a little scanner bot on the chance Meyerson had an alarm in the tunnel. The thing looked like a toy truck but in its nose was a dense collection of tech which swept the tunnel as they moved behind it.

When the scanner reached the end, it sent an all clear signal back to Luther.

"Tunnel's clean," said Luther.

"Copy," said Bane.

They arrived at the end of the tunnel and saw that there were more lights in the area.

Luther climbed up another iron ladder and felt a door at the top. He lifted it gently and it hit something hard and heavy.

"Something's sitting on the entrance door," said Luther. "If I tip it, it may crash."

"It can't be anything too cumbersome," said Bane. "He'd have to get it off the door quickly."

"I'll need a look around."

Luther took out a small telescoping camera and pushed it under the edge of the door. He panned around and saw a dank looking basement and wine cellar.

There was no one in the room and on top of the door was a small table with a flat bottom. He checked the area and saw that there was nothing on the table or near it. It was just there to hide the door.

Luther shoved the door open and the table fell to one side. He and Bane scrambled into the cellar quickly, guns out in case someone heard the noise. They replaced the table then waited.

No one came and no alarm sounded. They swept the cellar and it was clear. From their map of the place, the cellar staircase went up into a big pantry, which was a quick step into a kitchen which was off the pool area. There was a side door to the pantry that led to a den and into the larger house itself.

"They'll be two men watching the party," said Bane. "The third will be roving."

Suddenly, the door to the cellar opened. Luther and Bane moved to the rear of the room and hid in the shadows behind a wine rack. The door remained open and they heard the sound of a party and music.

A small man came in and ran to a shelf, removed a can of something and then ran back up the stairs.

"That sounded like a lot of people," said Luther.

"How long are we going to wait?" asked Bane.

"We should do the extraction after the party. It might be in the early hours of tomorrow."

They settled back into the dark corner and waited. This was definitely the most boring part of the job, Luther thought. His mind flashed quickly back to Greece and the warehouse where he'd spent days waiting.

"We can strap Meyerson to that dolly over there," said Luther. "That'll make the transport easier when we leave."

"We should have killed that Israeli," said Bane absently.

"Probably," said Luther. "After all, he was going to kill you if he'd gotten the order."

"Not too late. I put a tracker on him."

"If he's got any skill, he's found out by now," said Luther.

"Maybe."

They sat in the shadows for hours, interrupted once by two staffers who dropped into the cellar to have sex.

It was awkward as Luther and Bane listened to them grunt and moan against a far wall.

From what Luther could see, one of the women was twenty or so and the other woman was about ten years older. They went at it on a blanket on the floor like two teenagers, scissoring each other, moaning and whispering.

It was very erotic to Luther and he could not help but to get a little excited. He thought of Cari, her body and casual dismissiveness. God help him if he ever felt nothing from a spectacle like this.

Bane tapped Luther on the arm and smiled at him like a kid watching porn. She angled her head to get a better look all the while grinning.

When the couple was done, the older woman left first and then after a moment, the young girl walked up the stairs.

"Hot, huh?" said Bane.

"Yeah," said Luther a little distracted by something.

"Maybe I will give that pilot some," said Bane. "I do like Rome."

Luther was silent. They had to get their package and get out of here. That was their first priority.

"You go first," he said to Bane.

Bane slept first and then Luther tried but could not fall asleep. At two in the morning, Luther's watch issued an alarm and he and Bane sprang into action.

They pulled on masks and then surfaced in the pantry and Luther cut left and Bane right. He was going to neutralize the roving guard and Bane was to retrieve the package.

Luther spotted the roving guard before Bane hit the stairs to the bedrooms. The guard was coming out of a bathroom, zipping up his pants. He spotted Luther just as the dart hit him in the throat. Luther followed behind the projectile and made sure the man was down. The tranquilizer would keep him out for a good hour or so.

He and Bane had contemplated killing all the guards. It would send a signal to the police not to look for Meyerson. In the end, it was more trouble they didn't need. No one was going to see Meyerson again. No need to be barbaric.

The other two guards walked a perimeter around the back of the place. As they crossed paths, Luther cut them both down with his dart gun.

There were two guards in the front of the place and if they did a check in, all hell would break loose. They had to get out now, he thought.

"Got a problem," Luther heard Bane say in his ear. "Coming."

Luther ran up the stairs and found Bane standing in a doorway. Inside the room, Luther saw two people asleep in the bed. One of them was the thirty-year-old woman they'd watched having sex in the wine cellar. The other was Meyerson.

"What is it?" asked Luther, realizing that Meyerson's girlfriend was bisexual and having an affair with one of their staff most likely.

"I knocked them both out," said Bane, "but Meyerson has a room alarm on him. So does the lady here."

Bane pointed up and Luther saw a small machine above the door.

"He's got a tracker bracelet on," said Bane. "He leaves, the alarm sounds. We take it off, the alarm sounds."

"We gotta go," said Luther. "Grab him. The thing probably has a twenty or thirty yard range,"

Bane pulled Meyerson out of the bed. Luther grabbed the detector and pulled it from the wall. The device and the wires came out. Luther pulled it into the hallway and walked with it as it split the wall. He stopped at the head of the stairs.

Bane followed, dragging Meyerson behind her.

"This will buy us some time," said Luther.

Luther grabbed Meyerson and moved quickly down the stairs. They were all the way in the pantry when the alarm went off.

The forward guards would check in for a few seconds, then call it in. They had maybe twenty minutes to get out.

Luther and Bane strapped their package to the dolly and dropped him down the tunnel using a length of rope. Luther ran as fast as he could with the man behind him.

It took them both to lift him out of the tunnel at its end. They could see police lights coming to the mansion as they moved toward the house next door. Luther moved speedily and only dropped Meyerson once.

When they got to the house, they found the light on and a man standing outside the home with a shotgun looking around.

"They must have heard the sirens," said Luther.

"I got him," said Bane.

She ran to the man and put him down with a kick to the temple. Unfortunately, the gun went off.

Luther moved to the garage and placed Meyerson in the back of an SUV. Bane climbed in next to Meyerson.

The car had a push button ignition and Luther took out a device that quickly scanned the car's code. He started up the car and drove away with the lights off.

As they got to the main road, Luther pulled off the road as a line of police cars roared by.

"Well, that was sloppy as hell," said Bane. She moved forward to climb into the cab, only to see Luther facing her, holding two guns pointed at her.

One was the dart gun and the other was the P99.

The two friends looked at each other for what seemed a long time. Luther locked on her eyes. Each of the skilled assassins understood what this meant. Luther now knew something that Bane had attempted to hide. She could lie but he would kill her and if she confessed, it was likely the same would happen but not certain.

"When did you know?" asked Bane.

"Choose your next words carefully, Sharon," said Luther. "What is this really about?"

"I'm not working for the U.S. government," said Bane, "at least not the one you know. I came to get Meyerson for some people who operate without any official backing of the U.S."

"Enemies of the U.S.?"

"No."

"They what are they?" asked Luther.

"Complicated."

"So, you didn't stumble upon Meyerson, you were trying to find him."

"Yes."

"Why him?" asked Luther and his tone told Bane that the same rules applied as before. Lie and die.

"Because…" she hesitated for just a second. "I'm almost sure that Meyerson was supposed to die on 9-11 and he didn't because he knew it was going to happen."

"Bullshit," said Luther. "Truther conspiracy crap."

"Then how did Meyerson know to leave and why did he disguise himself as a fireman? Someone tipped him and he's been using that and other information to either extort money from certain individuals who are tired of paying or to bargain for this life."

It was not easy to shock Luther but he was. He took just a second to process and then it all made sense, letting him catch her following him, having him take out a man who she clearly knew was trailing her.

She needed him to get Meyerson and then she would extract Meyerson or kill them both, leaving Luther to take the blame.

Luther fired and Bane's body rolled next to their captive.

7

TripStick

Sharon Bane would never know that her interest in the lesbian couple in Meyerson's wine cellar had been the last clue Luther needed to be sure that she had deceived him.

He could believe that she had toyed with him in Paris when she let him discover her tail or even that she could not take out a simple surveillance agent on her own.

It was all a rather silly damsel act when he thought about it but that was why he had been fooled for so long. He was a man and Sharon and he did have this very subtle attraction and also, she had been a friend.

But her effort to look interested in the lesbian sex had bothered him. Sharon Bane did not like gays. This was a secret that only Luther and maybe a few others knew. Bane had no idea that this was her reputation at the agency.

Over the years, she had not been able to hide the looks in her eyes when gay agents and contacts were around. To most people, it was nothing, a twitch, a second of something in her eyes and expression but to Luther, to an agent, it was a flaw, a tell, a part of her personality that she had failed to successfully cover.

Bane had been raised in a conservative home in the south and it was hard to terminate all of your home training. She was enlightened but in her heart, there was still a core belief that homosexuality was wrong and against God and country.

Bane hid this from most people. She was good but Luther was better. When she feigned interest in the lesbians, her words and her face were excited but she had plain disgust in her eyes. And if she was faking that, it meant she was lying to him. And if she was lying, then she was dirty.

Luther had shot Bane with the dart gun and then taken her and Meyerson both to the safehouse he and Bane had procured for the mission, prepped them for interrogation and bound them back to back in chairs.

Meyerson and Bane's hands were bound in front of them and tied to their waists. He didn't want them to untie one another. He had no way of knowing if they were working together, which was one of the scenarios in his head.

Luther had also made tripsticks for both of them as well. A tripstick is a small charged weapon that was placed between the legs of a captive and hard linked to the wrists. If either of them pulled their knees apart, pressed them together too closely or moved their hands too far, it would fire a projectile into their femoral artery, severing it and they would be dead in less than a minute.

He had not made one in a long time and he hoped he had the calibrations right, otherwise, it was going to be a very messy day.

Meyerson awakened first. He was in good shape for a man his age. He was just under six feet and was balding. His muscular frame suggested he was on a steroid or HGH program.

That made sense, Luther thought. Meyerson was not a regular field agent but he had probably learned to defend himself and needed to stay in shape.

Meyerson tried to look around, he stopped when he saw the tripstick between his legs. He knew what it was and he grew very still.

His back was to Luther, who faced his old friend Bane. She was still unconscious but Meyerson could sense another person.

"Who are you?" asked Meyerson, his voice sounding strained. "I guess that's a stupid question. How about, what do you want?"

Luther said nothing for a long while. He was already working an hour ahead of this moment. In his mind, both of them were dead and he was getting rid of the bodies. Meyerson was easy but how did he get rid of Bane if he killed her?

And since Bane was dirty, he knew the clock was running on him. Her people would come soon.

This whole situation stank and he was still a little mad that Bane had played him for so long. This was the moment, if he answered, then it meant that he would not kill them for now at least.

"E-1," said Luther finally.

"Then why am I still alive?" said Meyerson quickly.

The quickness of his answer told Luther that Meyerson's immediate plan was to keep Luther talking, trying to get as much info as he could. No agent could ever forget all of his training, Luther thought absently.

And then he remembered that Meyerson was some kind of legend for interrogation resistance.

"You already know the answer to that," said Luther.

"Something went wrong," said Meyerson. "And what is that?"

"*I* am not dead," said Luther.

Meyerson's back straightened a little. This was good news to him.

"Then you should let me go and forget about this," said Meyerson. "The people responsible will be coming. No need for all of us to die. Nice tripstick, by the way. Haven't seen one in decades."

"If I got this right, running is not an option," said Luther. "I have questions and you would do well to answer them truthfully."

"I took the truth recognition course at Quantico," said Meyerson.

"Not as good as the one we take. Who caused the attacks on 9-11? Give me a crazy conspiracy theory and you know how this ends."

Meyerson now sagged a little in his chair. His training was evident but it was not holding.

"I need to use the bathroom," said Meyerson.

"Do it in your pants."

"I'll answer but I have questions, too."

"I can break a rib or a finger or I can take a hammer to your toes, said Luther. "All rather barbaric, but effective. You are in no position to negotiate with me."

Meyerson sighed again. "The planes were terrorists. Not just Al-Qaeda but several splinter groups of what is now ISIS." He took a long breath then said: "There are always plots against the U.S., but this one had very determined people. And on our side some powerful people knew or suspected it would happen."

"Traitors," said Luther. His voice was low.

"If you say so," said Meyerson. "The notion that our government did it was classic counter-disinformation. Designed to tap into the distrust people have for their nation. The truth was far more frightening."

This made some sense to Luther. He never bought the official story and the conventional conspiracy nut story that it was our own government, was silly to him but an operational coup, that was as old as the Roman Empire.

There had always been rogue elements within the U.S. and several failed coup attempts, including the only one with recorded evidence in 1934 against FDR.

The delicate balance of capitalism and democracy often gave power to a few men who had greater ambitions than wealth and citizenship.

It also explained why the government was so cagey and secretive about what happened and why The 9-11 Commission Report was so full of holes. Americans would have panicked if they knew there was a powerful rogue element in the hierarchy of government.

"Traitors who sided with foreign interests," said Luther. "That would ruffle a few feathers."

"More and more the world is about companies, we are money and power, not nations," said Meyerson. "The Chinese own the Waldorf Astoria, Chevys are made in Brazil. Patriotism, *Americanism* means nothing to these men."

When faced with the incredible, most people fold, their minds immediately looking for safe havens against the capacities of humanity, Luther thought. This is why when a shooter kills children, we talk about gun control and not the systemic problems of our society. This was why almost every other atrocity ended in useless discussions of race and politics and not humanity or reality.

In E-1, one of the first thing an agent learns is to never be shocked by the incredible or the implausible because that terrain was the ground that you would live upon for the rest of your life.

He believed Meyerson, or at least he believed that *Meyerson believed* what he was saying. Which left only one question.

"Okay then, where is it?" asked Luther. "Your proof."

"Back in the states."

"What is it?" asked Luther.

"Notes, dates memos with signatures, pictures and just a few minutes of very damning video that was taken using an experimental camera."

"Why not expose them?" asked Luther.

"My family, my son."

"As opposed to an entire nation? I'm not buying that."

"I've grown fond of living, agent," said Meyerson. "And there was no one who would have believed me back then."

"Why did they do it?" asked Luther.

"Why does anyone do something along this magnitude: power and not just any old power, world dominating authority."

"But we had to know," said Luther. "The agency would have had some idea of it."

"Yes but what did we know? We had a rumor that billionaires were gathering to talk about a global future where the U.S. figured prominently. And then there's a rumor that they want to change America's view politically. So what else is new?"

"So who were the insiders?" asked Luther.

"That's why I'm here," said Meyerson. "I have the names. They were referred to as The Core, seven men of enormous wealth and power who had the means to change the world."

Bane came to at this moment and Luther felt it. She shifted in her chair and was probably already thinking what she would do to get free.

Luther's training told him to kill her now in full view of Meyerson, to scare him into cooperation. If he didn't, Meyerson would sense weakness and Luther would be that much further from whatever the hell this was.

Luther took his P99 and placed the silencer on it.

"Why the ruse?" he asked Bane.

"You had to think it was all legit," said Bane, still a little groggy. "I couldn't have you compromising the mission by reporting it."

"I can be useful!" said Meyerson hearing the familiar click of a silencer. "No need to do anything rash here."

"You should be quiet now," said Luther. To Bane, he asked: "Why would you do this? Money? Surely, you haven't fallen that far."

"What difference does it make, said Bane grimly. "You're in the presence of the last boyscout, Meyerson. Luther Green can't be bought, bribed or bullied. Right now, he's thinking that he should definitely kill me but maybe not you. Depends on what you've told him."

"Look," said Meyerson, "No one has to die here."

"That's not true," said Bane. "Is it, Luther?"

Luther was silent and it felt like death was already in the room, thick and patient.

"This is why I never liked field work," said Meyerson.

"He says 9-11 was an operational coup by a rogue element," said Luther. "Why is he still a threat?"

"You don't get it," said Bane. "The rogue element as you call it didn't lose that day. They won."

Luther was struck silent. It had never occurred to him that this could be the case. It had been fifteen years since the attack and there was no change in America.

"Rabbit hole," said Meyerson. "We get attacked and while we're all reacting to it, the course of the nation changes from defender to aggressor. Everything changes from the space program to the price of soda. One war, two wars, war all the time and pretty soon, no one can remember what we used to be like."

"But even that was probably within the plan," said Luther way ahead of him. "The mission, the operation would cover all contingencies."

"Yes," said Meyerson. "This was just part one of the plan. Part two is in full swing and I am now more than an irritation. I'm a loose end."

Luther turned the weapon on Bane.

"Name your controller," he demanded.

"Why?" asked Bane. A good agent gives disinformation when captured. "If we talk, we also mix it with the truth."

"Humor me," said Luther leveling the gun.

Bane began to talk.

She was right, Luther thought. It made no sense for her to tell him the complete truth. She was dead and so, if she was telling the truth, then she was using it to—

Suddenly, Bane shoved the chair to one side, lifting her hand as much as she could in front of her.

Luther lunged for Meyerson and slapped his trip-stick upwards as it fired away from him. At the same moment, there was a loud pop and Bane issued a scream.

Distract was the word in Luther's head. Bane would be telling the truth to distract him while she figured out a way to beat the tripstick.

Luther went to her and saw that the charge from her tripstick had fired and hit her hands, partially severing her binds. But it went through her wrist and into her chest. Blood gushed from her, soaking her from the chest wound. He'd used a pretty big charge in the stick and it had worked.

"Foolish," said Luther.

"Almost angled it right," said Bane. "They'll come after you for what you know. Be smart. Cross over, Luther. Can't win this game."

It was too late, Luther thought. She would be gone in a few minutes.

"Hey!" said Meyerson. "What the fuck is this?"

Luther heard cars pulling up outside. He went to the window and saw two SUV's. Bane had not reported back to her people on time and they were coming.

Bane yelled in pain as the charge ate through her. Luther went to his utility bag and withdrew a hypo and quickly filled it with a compound. He slammed it into Bane's thigh and watched as the pain on her face turned into relief, then she smiled a little.

"Wow…" she said as her eyes fluttered and closed for the last time.

Luther pulled Meyerson up and released him.

"We have to go or we will both be dead," said Luther. "Your only bet is with me."

They could not go out of the building's front or back or even the emergency route he and Bane had come up with. He could not trust that she had not given that away to her people.

But a good agent always plans for himself and Luther had done so. He and Meyerson sneaked out of the building through a sub-basement and came up through a sewer grating on the next street. Their feet were covered in sewage but they calmly walked away as the building was stormed by the agents.

"This Core, how many are left?" asked Luther as they rounded a corner.

"I don't know," said Meyerson.

"What are they planning?"

"I don't know for certain."

"How did you extort money from them and not get caught?" asked Luther. "They can trace cash."

"Money," said Meyerson, "is the most secure thing in the world. We cheat everything but we play by the rules when it comes to money. I used accounts in five different countries and one criminal laundering site which uses bitcoin. I end up losing half but it's worth it to stay alive."

Luther saw a valet park a car in a lot and run off. He and Meyerson went to the little Puegeot and got in. Luther got the code for the starter and drove away.

"I need the location of your evidence," said Luther sternly.

"The day before 9-11, a friend of mine and his family were murdered in Michigan. That man, Robert Cantini was buried in a shallow grave in Detroit. I was given evidence on the people plotting against the U.S. and sent it to him in an old DRU drive. He was instructed to make no copies and put it in his leg."

"Did you say *in* his leg?" asked Luther

"Yes Robert had a prosthetic leg, army issue," said Meyerson. "He lost the bottom part of his leg in the army. He always angled himself so that the leg was away from people. He was ashamed of it. Stopped wearing brown shoes for some odd reason. Said people noticed any shoe that wasn't black. Annoying habit that I came to like about him."

Meyerson's memory process often caused him to rattle off details that most people would never recall.

Luther would have to get used to it. It was information overload but he had a talent that might come in handy.

"So how did they find out about Cantini?" asked Luther as he rounded a sharp corner.

"They didn't," said Meyerson. "It was just bad luck. Cantini worked for Strategic Air Command in a new division that President Clinton started."

"Right," said Luther. "A.T.A.S., the Air Threat Alert System. It was a beta program routing all info out of Michigan, Texas and Oregon. Buried in a spending bill as I recall."

"Cantini was killed so that no warning would go out on the planes when they went off course and headed toward targets. Michigan would have sent those alerts."

"Then there's no way he could have told you," said Luther.

"No," said Meyerson, the sadness evident in his voice. "The same people that hit Cantini were the ones who sent me to the towers that morning to die."

"Who tipped you off then?" asked Luther. He needed to keep Meyerson talking, keep the info going.

"Carl Jennings, a DOD man. Jennings was sent to Michigan to backwash the man they'd hired to kill Cantini, which he did."

"He tipped you off and then he was killed," said Luther knowingly.

"When they realized I wasn't dead, Jennings told me where Cantini's body was then he told me to run."

"How did they kill Jennings?" asked Luther a little curious now.

"Jennings had a partner," said Meyerson. "That would have been the easiest way to do it. They followed the hitter while he disposed of the bodies. When he was finished, they took him out. Jennings may have been killed that very night for all I know. We never found him. He just disappeared. Terrible for his family."

"And you skipped the country. So, how do you know it's still there?"

"I checked on it from time to time. The police found the body in 2007 but Cantini was buried with the leg intact, military burial."

"And this Jennings, he was a member of The Core?"

"No," said Meyerson. "He didn't have nearly enough wealth. I've always suspected that one of the members of the Core fed Jennings information but I can't prove it."

"How did you know they sent Bane to kill you?" asked Luther.

"I didn't know it was her but someone was looking for me and they hit the usual sources when I travel. I've hired Ravi before because he's good. I was just covering my ass. Ravi, is he—?"

"What about your lady friend?" asked Luther ignoring the question.

"Jouet? If she is not dead," said Meyerson, "she knows to disappear tomorrow. What are we going to do?"

"Time for us to disappear, too," said Luther.

8

Meyerson

Luther and Meyerson ditched their car and were soon back on their feet. It was always safer to move by foot. Luther moved so quickly that Meyerson was having trouble keeping up.

He'd salvaged everything he could in the way of munitions and money but for now, he was rogue and operating by those rules.

As they moved, Luther was treated firsthand to Meyerson's gift. He recounted the entire last month of his life to Luther in startling detail and remembered every twist and turn in the streets of his new hometown. He even recounted to Luther a conversation they'd had years ago, something that Luther had to take at face value because he had no recollection of it.

"Can't win this game."

Bane's statement haunted him. She took some secrets to the grave but she had tried to help him in the end.

Her people were powerful and ruthless. They would not stop until they had Meyerson. It would be easy for Luther to hand him over and negotiate for his own life. Bane knew that.

But just because a man kills for a living doesn't mean he doesn't have a code, Luther thought. He swore to protect his nation from all threats foreign and domestic. These men, whoever they were, had crossed the line and so they would have to kill him before he got Meyerson's information and leveraged them with it, just like he'd done with the President.

Luther looked for an apartment they could use. He needed to make some communications but could not risk using his own equipment right now.

After an hour or so, Luther finally found a suitable place to break into. It was above a little shop on what would be a busy street come daybreak. Luther easily scaled the building from the rear and disabled the alarm.

Luther quickly checked the place to make sure it was unoccupied. It was. The apartment was a very nice converted loft. The decor was rich with soft leathers and expensive looking furniture and fine art on the walls. Meyerson marveled at the paintings, calling out the artists by name.

Suddenly, the house phone rang. Luther saw the caller ID was a security service. There must have been an auxiliary backup to the main alarm.

"Shit," Luther said.

He answered the phone knowing that if he didn't, they would send a dispatch and call police.

"*Olá?*" said Luther in his best Portuguese. It was a difficult language and not one of his best.

"Your back up system has been turned on," said the operator in the same language. Password?"

Luther looked around in a slight panic and then he saw the password written on a post-it by the phone. A very silly thing to do, he thought.

"*Picada*," said Luther.

"Thank you and now if you have your Emergency Security Code ID please."

Luther was stumped. Now the panic was real.

"I uh, it must be somewhere here," said Luther. "I am a temporary."

"No problem, I can wait."

This meant if he didn't get it, they'd send a unit and maybe police just to be sure and to cover their asses for insurance.

Just then, Meyerson held out a piece of paper with a long set of numbers on it. Luther repeated the numbers.

"Thank you," said the security worker. "Will you need repairs?"

"Yes, I think. I am housesitting. You can send a man tomorrow?"

"What time?"

"Oh, late afternoon if you don't mind."

"Five thirty?"

"Yes, very good."

"Okay it is set. Have I satisfied your needs this evening?"

"Yes, yes," said Luther faking a laugh. "I do not know much about this, but yes."

The service person laughed also then ended the call.

"Where did you get that number?" asked Luther.

"It was on the inside of the alarm cover you found," said Meyerson. "I glanced at it when we came inside."

"A glance?"

"Well, I looked," said Meyerson feeling a little embarrassed for some reason. "It clearly said *ID* on it."

"Good job," said Luther. In his head, he was marveling at Meyerson's powers. He had to remember that this was no ordinary man.

"The man who lives here is a local actor," said Meyerson pointing to a framed magazine cover. "He does a TV comedy show I enjoy, *Doctor Jungle*. He's probably shooting in Africa right now."

"Good," said Luther. "Let's hope he doesn't come home suddenly."

Luther found a very nice communications system in an office. Luther set up his computer and sent encrypted messages until he was in his backdoor at the agency.

Every good agent had a secret backdoor to the government for just such emergencies. Soon, Luther was on a fuzzy vid chat with Cari.

"Busy boy," said Cari looking tired. "If you are contacting me this secretly, then you have been up to something bad."

"Missing man in Portugal," said Luther.

"I heard about that," said Cari. "I assume you need to leave our little continent and that's why you are calling."

"Yes," said Luther.

Just then, Meyerson passed Luther a piece of paper which asked him to check on his girlfriend.

"Have you heard anything about a woman named Jouet Pillar?" asked Luther.

Cari took a moment, then: "She was found at the scene of the kidnapping," said Cari. "She is being questioned by police."

Meyerson sighed in relief at this.

"So, can you help me?" asked Luther.

"Yes," said Cari. "I will send instructions by the usual channel. You will have to make it for a day in order for me to get to you."

"Understood," said Luther.

"There is no order for your capture," said Cari. "You should be careful then."

"Yes, if they are not looking for me openly," said Luther, "then they are doing it secretly. Were there any reports of casualties?"

Luther was trying to find out if Bane's body had been recovered. If it was, then her handlers might be stepping off the mission. If it wasn't, then the chase was on.

"No," said Cari. "But we are on a low alert."

Luther was silent. He had his answer. Bane's people had cleaned her body and the safehouse. She was not working for the agency but someone much more dangerous.

"It will be hard to extract you," said Cari. "If anyone suspects you, they will be watching me."

"But you can beat that," said Luther.

"Of course, I can."

Luther ended the call and then started doing searches on the CIA's server. He really wished he had a Tech and Weapons Advisor. He or she would be able to cut through a lot of the bullshit security.

"I hope Jouet is okay," said Meyerson.

"I'd say it's likely if she doesn't arouse suspicion," said Luther. "How much did she know about you?"

"Nothing," said Meyerson. "All of our precautions were taken because of my wealth."

"Then she will be okay and the local police will wait for a ransom," said Luther.

"What about the federal people, the spooks?"

"They will be watching her," said Luther. "So you can't call or contact her and if you access your money without high level protection, they will know it's you."

"What are we going to do for money then?" asked Meyerson.

"I'm not sure yet," said Luther. "I have some but we will need more, especially if our extraction point is a long way off, which I suspect it will be."

"This guy is pretty well off," said Meyerson. "We could sell one of these paintings. That Hernan Bas there looks like an original."

"Too messy," said Luther. "I need to find out how much trouble we are in. Look for something more easily exchanged. He might have a safe."

Meyerson moved off and began to look around. Luther hoped Meyerson had already catalogued just about everything in the place.

Meyerson's memory was more than just rote recollection, Luther thought. He had the ability to associate and draw conclusions as well, something they had all learned at Quantico and the agency.

"There are patterns of blue all over the place, the occupants favorite color obviously," he said. He looked through all of the pictures and mail and anything the actor had laying around.

Meyerson looked in all of the usual places for a safe. But there was nothing in the closets or the bedroom floor.

"Got something," he said to Luther.

Luther entered the bedroom, to find Meyerson standing by the bed.

"What is it?" asked Luther.

"All of the tables and stands here were made by the same company, Hillier-Strauss," he said. "They all have the company seal on it somewhere. Fine woods and excellent craftsmanship. All the tables are by this company, except one, the table in the bedroom is made by a different company but it looks identical to the one opposite it, which is a Hillier-Strauss. This one has a different name on it, Cogent.

Meyerson tilted it and found it to be almost immovable. It was wooden on the outside but there was something dense underneath. He checked it and found a latch that released a door revealing a safe with a computer interface.

"Nicely done," said Luther.

Meyerson quickly got some powder from the bathroom and sprinkled a light amount over the keys. Several of the keys had powder on then that clumped because human fingers and moisture had been on them. The code was from these keys.

"The main character from the TV show *Doctor Jungle* is Wallace Kuvic," said Meyerson.

"Try it," said Luther.

Meyerson entered the name. Nothing. He tried it backwards and the safe opened.

Inside, he found papers on all of the paintings. They were all originals. There were several expensive watches and stacks of euros and American dollars.

"Excellent," said Luther. "Why would he have so much money at home?"

"Drug addict and gambler," said Meyerson. "All his fans know that."

"I have some info," said Luther, "but it's not good."

They walked back to the actor's office area and Luther showed Meyerson his laptop.

"The agency knows Bane has been eliminated and they are checking on it. They will send a message to me because of our proximity. If I do not respond, they will assume I am dead as well and if they find I am not, I will be a suspect. The good news is, the agency is not in on Bane's betrayal."

"So, you go blind," said Meyerson. "Do we still call it that?"

"Yes," said Luther. I will give it some time, so they will think I am trying to piece it together."

"So, are we good to stay here, tonight?" asked Meyerson.

"I would love to," said Luther, "but it's too dangerous. We can't be sure if we have been made and it always pays to keep moving when you are running. We stay a few hours and then move. We have a day before we hear from my contact about extraction."

"Pity," said Meyerson.

Over a meal of beer and sandwiches, Luther compiled a plan to stay out of sight.

Meyerson looked worried, presumably about his girlfriend. Luther did not want to tell him that she might be killed but Meyerson had to know that.

"How did they get you to go into the towers that day?" asked Luther.

"I carried a set of instructions to a weapons dealer who posed as a financial specialist. I should have known something was wrong because anyone could have relayed this information. Anyway, Jennings called me that morning while I'm having coffee and tells me to get the hell out, to run. He sends an encrypted text with the other information. I excuse myself and I go. I get close to the lobby in an elevator and the first plane hits. It was like the Hand Of God. My elevator stalls and I climb out, leaving a very frightened woman. I make my way down toward the lobby and there is a frenzy on the stairs. By the time, I get to the bottom the first responders are there. And then, I swear to you, there is an explosion under us."

"Someone blew the supports in the sub basements," said Luther. "That was reported by some firemen, then later denied."

"Yes but I didn't know it then. I was scared as hell. I had an association of memories in my head by now and I knew I'd been set up. I knew if I came out, they'd catch me on a feed and I'd be dead in a day or two. I saw a fireman had fallen. He'd been hit by something and his coat and helmet was removed to let him breathe. I took his big coat and put it on along with his headgear, grabbed the nearest hysterical person and walked out."

"You were wearing your watch, a Rolex," said Luther smiling a little.

"No time to think about that," said Meyerson. "I made it out and went past the reporters. I took off. No one stopped me because they thought I was going for help. I went into a building, took off the outfit and ran like hell."

"You initiated your contingency plan?"

"Yes," said Meyerson. "I knew there would be no flights and so I headed to Florida. Took me a day."

"The President's brother," said Luther calmly. "Secret flights?"

"Lots of them. I grabbed one to the Bahamas. From there, it was a quick jump to the Caymans. I saw in the newspapers that a lot of people had made money in the stock market on companies adversely affected by the attacks and made a fortune. Then I knew for sure."

"Operational profit generators," said Luther. "Greed trumps secrecy every time."

"When I saw my name counted among the dead, I knew I was home free for at least a while."

"So, your family collected on your insurance?"

"Yes, but the wife didn't know about any of my secret holdings," said Meyerson. "We were already on the rocks but I was going to stay for the kids, you know."

"How much did it cost you to relocate?"

"Only a million or so," said Meyerson calmly. "I'd made a mint using inside information when I was with the government. I had holdings all over."

"So, when did you find out about The Core?" asked Luther.

"I knew about them before," said Meyerson looking rather grim. "They were up-and-comers, big time lobbyists, old money concerns but I didn't know they had any bigger ambitions. A multi-level op on that magnitude is a big deal."

"How did you keep them from killing you?" asked Luther.

"I let them know I had the damaging info," said Meyerson and now he looked like his mind was somewhere else.

"But if they found you, no one would have believed it right after the attacks," said Luther. "The media was swirling with conspiracies, all completely made up."

"Yes, so I knew I had to keep alive for at least a year until cooler heads prevailed, lawsuits were filed and most importantly, a commission formed."

Whenever there was a national tragedy that the people just could not handle, the government formed a commission in order to let people know action was being taken. This allowed for time to go by while anger and tension quelled. The JFK Commission was the most famous. But no commission report had ever found a single conspiracy or recommended action. The 911 Commission Report was no different.

"I lived in fear," Meyerson continued, "not sleeping, tired and on all kinds of meds. I just knew someone was going to walk up to me and put one behind my ear but it never happened. So, I set myself up here and hoped they'd agree to a detente."

"By then, we were at war," said Luther.

"Yes and I guess no one wanted to be bothered with the likes of me."

Meyerson drained his beer and suppressed a belch. He had that look like he wanted to drink more but was debating it.

"We get a little sleep, then should move," said Luther. "I'll pull the place apart a little to make the robbery look good. Then we have to stay safe for twenty-four hours."

"What are we going to do for a whole day?" asked Meyerson. "There are cameras all over the place."

"Travel to our meeting point," said Luther.

"And then?"

"I'll figure that out if we get out of Europe alive."

≈≈≈≈≈≈≈≈≈≈≈≈≈≈≈≈≈≈≈≈≈≈≈≈≈≈≈≈≈≈

PART TWO:

THE DOMESTIC GAME

"If an operation is threatened, you must
counter the threat with every non-lethal
action at your disposal. If these methods
fail, then you must eliminate everything
and everyone with a connection to the truth."

- Black Ops Manual

≈≈≈≈≈≈≈≈≈≈≈≈≈≈≈≈≈≈≈≈≈≈≈≈≈≈≈

9

Blind

Comporta, Portugal

A light rain fell like mist as Luther and Meyerson waited on the tiny airfield at night. They had moved west to the small costal city Cari had sent to Luther by encryption. The information came slowly but it was necessary as he was sure that the area was on an undercover alert.

The airfield had no official name but there was a sign that had a big blue *"XE"* on it. It was not on any map that Luther had ever seen but it was close to the ocean and you could fly out, without raising a lot of notice.

Luther and Meyerson sat on a bench under a light that Luther had disabled. Even though the place was remote, he did not want to attract any undue attention. Only two planes had landed and taken off into the night so far.

Traveling with Meyerson was more pleasant than Luther had hoped. Meyerson was quiet, followed orders well, and his Portuguese was very good.

They'd spent most of their allotted day on the road, using the money they'd stolen to buy rides from non-car service types. They kept to back roads and secondary towns and avoided all of the places they could be acquired.

Luther still did not fully trust Meyerson but he had no choice now. They were both on a mission not entirely of their making.

The inevitable communication from the government came to Luther that morning. As always, it bore no official department but carried the agency code.

His American contact wanted to know why he had not completed his final report and if he knew what had happened to agent Sharon Bane.

This was more evidence that something was amiss. Not even the agency knew what Bane had been up to.

Luther reported that he had gone blind. This was a field code that he had not used in a long time. It meant that he was in a collateral situation from his mission and could not report until he had more information. It also meant that his life was in danger and he was going off the grid.

The agency requested Luther to come in, which was not the normal response. Normally, they would say nothing and just wait or ask for a period of time for his next report. But this time, they insisted that he come in.

Luther said nothing. He ended the correspondence. He was now a blind agent in the field.

It occurred to Luther more than once that he could be a hero and just take Meyerson out. The problem was, Bane was right about him. He still believed in honor and if the U.S. was in danger, it was his job to protect it.

So, Luther did not check back with his American contacts for fear that the corruption was there as well. If Meyerson, Alex and Cari were right and something bad was brewing in the states, he could not count on his people right now.

Meyerson's disappearance had not made the news. This was the best evidence yet that Bane had been into something really bad. Wealthy men did not just disappear without a lot of noise.

"I hope we can trust your friend," said Meyerson.

"We don't have a choice," said Luther.

"She a love of yours? I'm guessing."

"Not anymore," said Luther seeing no reason to lie.

"At least I had a normal life for a while," said Meyerson.

Something was on Luther's mind, something which had been bothering him since the revelation and Bane's death.

"How did they do it?" he asked Meyerson. "The attack on 9-11."

"I wasn't in on anything," said Meyerson, "but after that day, I had some time to figure it out. It's all there if you are looking for it."

"That doesn't answer my question. How?"

"There are always plots against us, you know. Easy to let one progress, watch it and then let it happen if you are against your own nation."

"That doesn't explain the buildings," said Luther. "Why did they fall and why did Building Seven fall? It was never hit."

"They were blown, of course," said Meyerson calmly. "That information is all over the place. The newspapers, media outlets all reported explosions. It was only downplayed after because if there were explosions, that would lead to nasty questions. The public would know that something like this could not have been done by a few maniacs with box cutters."

"And so," said Luther, "while the actual terrorist attack is going on, this group, The Core, is planning a parallel operation to grab power post the event."

"Exactly," said Meyerson. "911 was a real terrorist attack but these guys used it opportunistically to make a bolder move."

"But people have been very suspicious of the event," said Luther, "and quite frankly, a lot of people do not believe the official story."

"But they are asking the wrong questions," said Meyerson. "They are looking at wars, military contracts, money and all the usual conspiracy crap. The real benefit has come in internal change. Not the Presidency, that job hasn't had any real power since JFK caught one. The people who run the government behind the scenes, the companies and international concerns like the WTO, IMF, Global Tech and the UN is where the real power is. After 911, that power shifted and a new group rose to power and now they call the shots."

"So both wars were misdirection?"

"Necessary and expensive but you don't change the world like you do a light bulb."

"You re-wire the whole damned house," Luther said grimly. "So whatever this Core is planning now must be a supplement to the first operation."

"And that's why your friend came to get me and kill you."

Luther was already wondering what the operation could be. He was still wrestling with the fact that for the last fifteen years, the government had been operating under the leaders of an operational coup.

Cari arrived an hour later via a small private jet which had taxied on a tarmac. Luther figured that this was their transport.

Cari moved over to them in her rain gear and for a second, Luther got a flash of urgency. He saw Cari pulling a weapon and shooting them both but not before telling him that she was in on Bane's ill-fated mission.

But she didn't. She just walked up to them and spoke with urgency.

"Good to see you, Luther" said Cari. "No introductions please. We don't have much time. You cannot go by plane. I received an H-11 alert this morning. All airports will be on watch here and probably in America."

"Then we need to go by sea if we can," said Luther. "How long will it take to arrange something?"

"I already did," said Cari. "It's not far from here but we will have to go all night. You leave in the morning but not for America. The ship will take you to Canada. From there, you are on your own."

"Canada?" said Meyerson. "We may have a border problem."

"We'll figure it out," said Luther. "Let's get moving."

They got into a car that Cari had arranged and drove away. It was an uneventful trip and Cari admonished Luther not to tell her anything about what had happened. If she were questioned later, she wanted to be honest when she said she didn't know anything.

She held his hand tightly as they moved. Luther appreciated that more than he could tell her.

By daybreak, they were boarding a cargo ship with about twenty other men and hundreds of containers.

There was an awkward moment but the pair did kiss goodbye. Luther could feel Meyerson watching.

"I would tell you to be careful," said Cari, "but I know you always are. So instead, I will say try not to kill too many people."

"I can't promise that," said Luther.

****

Ontario, Canada.

The cargo ship _Palinouros_, entered port in Canada's Hudson Bay under a clear sky. It had been a week since Luther and Meyerson had gotten aboard. They had blended in well with the other men, posing as transit company men for Lukkex Trading. Cari's cover had even afforded them nice living quarters along the way.

Meyerson had told Luther his whole life story during the trip. He'd been recruited out of high school and taken into the Army in the late 1970's. From there, he received an education in all things covert. His perfect memory vaulted him to the top of each class and eventually earned him a security clearance on the highest levels.

He became a Server after he delivered information that saved President George H.W. Bush from an assassination attempt.

After that, Meyerson was always on some secret mission, carrying information in his head to some powerful person or meeting. He did a stint for the IMF and made a fortune on the secrets he'd gotten on the currency markets.

He was planning a nice retirement as a lobbyist when 911 happened and he was marked for death.

The ship landed on the Ontario side of the bay. From there, Luther and Meyerson traveled by car south towards the Detroit border.

Cari's H-11 alert would mean that the border would be heavily guarded under an elevated terrorist threat. That meant they could not cross into the States by the bridge or tunnel.

Luther's training in urban missions told him that what was needed here were people who operated outside of the law.

The Detroit-Ontario border was one of the easier international borders to cross. A casual relationship between the two cities had been forged over the years. Still, illegal activity was always around and Luther needed to take advantage of it.

What he needed was smugglers who had a system going already. Even in times of peace and prosperity, there were always people who wanted more.

Luther and Meyerson broke into a house in an upperclass neighborhood and hacked their computer. It was a clean break, meaning that they would leave with no signs of the break in.

From there, he contacted Alex who had supplied him with a name he'd acquired from his various contacts.

"Cigarettes," said Alex. "More profitable than dope these days. There's a group that imports them across the border without tax or import fees."

"Good. We'll need to use them to get across," said Luther. "Do they have a system?"

"Of course," said Alex. "But I don't know what it is. "You'll have to test them."

Alex wired money which Luther took under an assumed name. Then he and Meyerson used their aliases to get to the dock where they found their contact waiting, a gangly man with wild hair named Leo.

"Money," said Leo gruffly. He wore a black peacoat and skull cap and his teeth were rotten and dark from chewing tobacco.

Luther handed him the money and watched as he counted it.

"The ship is named *The Gubner*," he said. "Dumbass name if you ask me. They know you're coming. Don't talk to anyone and when they tell you to move, just do it. Hesitate and I can't help you."

Leo walked with them to the ship, a luxurious looking white and blue yacht. Leo nodded to a man in a suit and Luther and Meyerson walked onboard.

The Captain, an older black man pointed them to a room. They entered and waited.

"I don't get this," said Meyerson. "Why would the owner of this ship smuggle anything?"

"It may not be him," said Luther. "It could be the captain but if this is a normal operation, then there has to be corruption with the border authorities. This river is a very small area and there's no way an ongoing smuggling operation would last without help."

They heard the sounds of a party but it was mostly below deck. This meant there was contraband being openly used.

The Captain turned the boat and headed across the river. At the halfway mark, Luther saw a Harbor Patrol boat pull alongside of them.

"Stop," demanded the Border Patrol over a loudspeaker.

The yacht's engines slowed then stopped and Luther heard the party people being huddled out.

"Fuck," said Meyerson. "They're made."

"I hope not," said Luther. "But if anything jumps off, be prepared to fight."

"Fight?" said Meyerson. "I don't fight."

The Captain opened the door soon thereafter, and summoned them.

"This way," he said.

Luther and Meyerson went topside to the rear of the yacht. There they saw another, smaller ship. A ramp had been set up and two men were loading boxes onto it, while the Border Patrol kept everyone entertained.

"Walk across," said the Captain.

Luther and Meyerson walked to the other ship. The men finished loading the boxes which contained cigarettes and then the smaller boat pulled away. The little smuggler ship sped off towards Detroit, following the Border Patrol.

When they got close to the dock in the U.S., Luther saw the smuggler's ship drop a small yellow container into the water. The Border Patrol picked it up and moved on.

The smugglers moved up river, past the city to their drop point. As they did, Luther saw the smuggler ship's Captain nod to the other man who moved to the back of the boat.

"Get ready," said Luther.

"For what?" asked Meyerson.

"These guys are going to try to rob us but I have a plan."

"Why?"

"Because they're criminals," said Luther. "And they think we are vulnerable. Who are we going to tell if they rob us?"

The smugglers pulled the boat into a tiny dock near the city. The smuggler captain, a beefy looking man in a Red Wings shirt moved toward them, when Luther pulled his gun.

"The fuck?" said the smuggler.

"Tell your man to put his gun down. Now," said Luther.

The smuggler nodded to the other man who removed a gun and put it on the boat's floor.

"Get it," Luther said to Meyerson.

Meyerson picked up the gun.

"Now take one of the boxes," said Luther. "Make it two."

"Motherfucker!" said the smuggler.

"Small price for what you had planned," said Luther. "You think I don't know when some fucks are going to jack me? You're lucky I don't shoot you."

"You and I are going to see each other again," said the Captain and when we do—"

Luther kicked him overboard.

"You, jump in," Luther said to the other man.

He jumped in the water. And while they struggled, Luther and Meyerson left the ship, taking two of the boxes of cigarettes with them.

10

The Boy From Belleville

Bellville, Michigan.

He looked at the order with excitement. Three years without a peep and suddenly he gets a red card. Someone up there was listening to his prayers, he thought.

The thing in his hand was actually off-white in color, its textured grooves looked like some kind of exotic art. Once he scanned it into his computer, it would interface with his Red Dog Security screen and then he'd know what was expected of him.

But it was a red card, he thought, so he already knew. The question was what unlucky man had run afoul of the devil.

Clement Black smiled, taking in a deep breath. He loved to breathe, unlike most people who took it for granted. He'd learned early on that deep breaths allowed you to strengthen your core and powered you. He wasn't into meditation or yoga or any of that sissy shit. He just knew breathing was good for you.

Clement sat in his little home office in Bellville, Michigan, where he lived and worked. It was a modest one-story job with a big adjacent lot where he had a small garden of flowers and vegetables.

His partner Trent, tended the garden and Clement let him because it kept him busy and happy. A happy mate was essential to him because he had so much he needed to keep hidden from the world.

First, there was his past. For years, he worked as a low level hitman for the local tough guys in Michigan. It was an unpleasant job but it was better than the daily beatings he and his sister had taken at the hands of their drug addict father. And when dad started selling them both to his druggie friends for sex, well, their life had become intolerable.

That was his first hit, the day he sent his dad to the great beyond by dropping a suspended motor on his head after he'd passed out in the garage. Messy, but effective.

He still dreamt about it from time to time, only in his dream, the motor would fall and his father would catch it, lifting it with demon-like strength. Then he would turn to a frightened Clement, his face filled with rage and murder.

"That's your ass, pink boy."

His father would take a lumbering step his way and then Clement would awaken, a precious breath caught in his trembling throat.

In reality that day, the motor dropped and it crushed the skull of J.D. Black, killing him instantly and freeing his children from their bondage.

When the police came to the run-down house and questioned the teenager, Clement had been calm as he sipped on one of his now dead father's forbidden Dr. Peppers, a drink that he could not have touched for fear of being killed just hours before.

He told the police how their mother was dead and it was just him, Justine and their father. And then he told them what he found after hearing a loud noise. He was cool, savoring the flavor of the drink and the sting of its carbonation.

One of the cops was suspicious. The kid was only fifteen, so he should have been pissing his pants. But there was no evidence of any foul play. The way it was suspended, that motor was just waiting to drop on someone, another cop had said.

This is when Clement knew he had a talent for disposing of people. His heart rate had not risen the slightest bit during the whole ordeal. All he would remember later was wanting another Dr. Pepper.

The state split them up, but three years later, he got Justine out of the system and they started living together.

By then, Clement was a known danger on the street in downriver Detroit. He'd grown into a hard, man with steel gray eyes and a slit of a mouth that made for a menacing face. And when he came looking for you, it was too late to beg or negotiate. You were finished.

Clement earned enough on the street to take care of himself and his sister while she finished school. Justine was a smart girl and Clement didn't want her brains to go to waste.

He was smart, too, although his particular aptitude involved violence.

Clement had had a banner year when a drug called Cold Medina had come to Detroit. The shit was killing people and the dealers all turned on each other. His services were used quite a bit and at the end of it, he had bought his first house.

After Justine went off to college in Denver, Clement devoted himself more fully to his occupation. He'd accepted that he was more comfortable with men and started looking for a relationship that was more secure than the one nighters and flings he was having.

Even though he'd been the victim of many forced couplings at the hands of his father's associates, he had always been attracted to men.

The state had sent him to counseling and the psychologist was nice enough but Clement had assured him that he had not been "turned" by his father's treachery.

Clement did not keep his sexuality a secret in the business and it cost him some, but criminals could not be picky when they needed an elimination and so Clement, the openly gay hitman, worked continuously for many years until he was caught on a murder charge.

He expected to go to prison but instead of some buzz cut boyscout prosecutor coming into his cell, he got a rather dangerous looking guy in a dark suit. He was from the government and he offered him a reduced sentence to join the military.

Clement took the deal and found himself in bootcamp with twenty other men and women on an island just off the coast of New Orleans. There, he was trained as what they called a Destroyer, a group of men whose only job was to go into hot areas and kill everything breathing.

He and his band of men worked the Afghan and Iraq Wars under coded names. They were not allowed to socialize with the other men though often they assisted in extreme interrogations with the spooks who were always around.

Clement loved his job. His desire for violence and blood had only grown since learning all the different ways you could kill a man.

After the war, Clement had a full pardon for his crimes. He'd applied for a position with the CIA's secret division. He was told that none existed but he expressed interest enough times that he received an anonymous letter for an evaluation.

Clement Black was turned down for the division called E-1 due to his psych evaluation. He didn't understand this and was angry but he surmised that you had to be some kind of kiss-ass to get in.

He went to work instead for Red Dogg, a private security firm run by ex-military that specialized in working with multinational corporations and government lobbyists.

Clement made a lot of money working for Red Dogg, enough that he retired at the ripe old age of thirty-nine. He settled back in Michigan where Justine now lived and worked as a teacher.

He moved to Belleville because as a kid, they'd pass through the sleepy town and it always looked like a safe haven.

He met his partner there, who had sold him a nice suit. When they met, Trent had gushed over how good he looked in it.

Clement settled down and opened a successful hardware supply business, catering to retail and construction. Clement didn't do much. He left the business to Trent and the fancy boys with college degrees.

Life could have gone on peacefully, if it were not for two very important things in his life. He had been kept on a retainer by Red Dogg, who still had strong ties to the government and needed him from time to time.

The other thing was his occupation as a part-time serial murderer.

Clement Black's appetite for blood had not just gone away with retirement. He had a deep anger inside that could only be quelled by the ending of a worthless life.

This had worked out fine as a criminal hitman and government Destroyer. Even with Red Dogg, he had roughed up and eliminated scumbags off the books. But as a respectable retiree, he had almost lost his mind.

After realizing that he had to do something to quell the rage, Clement had started going into Detroit, looking for trouble. It was not hard to find but any homeboy that stepped to him found himself talking to St. Peter that same day.

No one cared about the worthless lives in Detroit and over the years, he had taken out quite a few of them. He was averaging about one every six months or so. Just enough to keep him calm.

His kills took time because he had to get rid of the bodies in a way that would not invite some smart ass cop to play detective.

Disposing of a dead body was hard but he had become very proficient in this skill. Being in the hardware and construction business also helped as it was easy to buy huge amounts of acids, solvents and corrosives without suspicion. It was also useful to know where people were building around town. There were pieces of local vermin in foundations, concrete columns and houses all over the tri-county area.

He knew people would think he was sick but really he was just doing a job that other people didn't want to do.

He had really enjoyed the TV show *Dexter*. It was a funny show about a serial killer who killed other serial killers. In reality, people like him were very rare. If you were lucky enough to find a real serial murderer, he'd probably be the only one in your state.

General assholes were another situation. There were plenty of them in the world, like his father. Clement could spot them a mile away and if he could, he'd release them.

There were so many of these worthless human beings, leeching on society, doing nothing and just waiting to harm someone.

His very first kill when he'd come back to Michigan was what people thought was a homeless man but Clement knew better. He saw the man hanging around the local playground, watching the kids. He never saw him talk to or approach them but why wait? Sooner or later he would.

But the homeless man never got a chance. Clement had come into the city at night and waited for him. When the target turned up with another homeless man, Clement had followed them and when they separated, he'd taken the man, strangled him and dropped him into a hole that was filled with concrete the next day.

Trent had made shepherd's pie that day and he'd had a big portion when he returned home.

His third kill drew a news story and so Clement had turned his attentions away from the city for a while. A quick trip up north and he found another waiting victim and then he headed south later that year.

He'd even gone out of state a time or two, knowing that this would help clear any pesky police on his trail.

Clement never killed the same way twice and chose victims of all races. Some he'd strangle, others he'd stab or suffocate. He didn't like to shoot but always carried a gun.

And to go with his hobby, Red Dogg would send an assignment every once in a while. It started with little things, anonymous intimidation and then Clement graduated to domestic off-the-books eliminations. The payment (in addition to his retainer) was always great and he never asked if the target deserved it.

He'd only gotten three of these in his retirement. One was a Colonel who was going to testify about military contracting irregularities.

The second was a federal prisoner who had been allowed to escape and thought he was going to Canada. He ended up in the fuel housing of a freighter to Norway.

The last one was three years ago, when Clement had traveled to Cleveland and killed a state senator in a staged mugging.

He scanned the red card and brought up the image. He went to his secure sight and placed the image into the interface. The program opened. Clement smiled. He had another elimination. His mind began to race with how he would do it. He'd just gotten a big batch of sulfuric he was going to resell. That would be good, he thought.

Suddenly, there was a knock on the door. It jerked him out of his reverie.

"Come," said Clement.

Trent entered. Clement switched his screen to a business spreadsheet as he did.

"Don't forget we have the Hannahs tonight," said Trent.

"I didn't," said Clement.

"Why do you look at those things? You never understand them," said Trent, looking over his shoulder.

"Just trying to learn," said Clement. "What's on the menu?"

Trent was a great cook and had graduated from a culinary academy in Ann Arbor last year. Since then, he was all about the cuisine. He even made cooking videos that were quite popular online.

"Fillet and tiger prawns in madeira wine reduction, mixed greens and key lime for dessert."

"I'm gonna have to run to Florida to work that off," said Clement.

"It's actually pretty light," said Trent"and you never gain weight. I won't let you."

Trent left and Clement went back to his red card screen. He continued reading the assignment and was puzzled. Usually, they knew where his target was. This time, all he saw was two blurry sketches with the designation:

On foot in the city and very dangerous.
Sat imaging and tracking to come.
Find and eliminate. Threat level high.

Clement sat up straighter at this. There were four basic levels of a target's lethal capacity, the lowest being a civilian and highest being a dangerous criminal or a man with deadly training.

Clement printed the black and white sketches of Meyerson and Luther. There were no actual pictures of the pair, something else that was unusual. One was black and looked big. The other was white, middle aged and bald. Hardly badasses, he thought casually.

From the kitchen he heard the sound of Amy Winehouse, which meant Trent was beginning the early prep for his meal. He smiled. His life was very good and this little Red Dog assignment would be a nice diversion.

Clement looked at the threat assessment again. *High.* One or both of these men was considered dangerous. Probably the black one. He was younger, bigger.

No matter, Clement thought, there was no one more dangerous than he was.

11

Hickey

Detroit, Michigan.

Luther and Meyerson had no trouble selling the cigarettes. The city had changed but the black market had not. They dumped the contraband at a gas station whose owner almost danced at the site of the stolen merchandise.

Luther only took the cigarettes so the smugglers would remember them as local thieves and not anything else that might arouse suspicion.

Detroit was coming out of the largest municipal bankruptcy in history and now had a white mayor for the first time in over 40 years.

Gentrification was already underway but the city's neighborhoods were still ravaged by blight, crime and a half century of urban pathology and neglect.

Meyerson took easily to their new environment. Luther wondered if years away had made him fearful or if he harbored standard prejudices. A good agent understood that race and class were just tools that were used to separate common interests to protect the status quo. A millionaire could kill you as easily as a dope dealer and was more likely to get away with it.

They walked at a quick pace down Mack Avenue making sure to look away from any establishments with outside cameras.

Luther's European contacts were right about one thing, something negative was brewing in the U.S. Over the last five years, domestic violence and racially inspired hate crime had risen. To lay people, this was just more evidence of the assholes in society and it played well to their pride, bigotry and hypocrisy. To an agent, it had all the hallmarks of a grand scheme, an operation with a predicted ending.

But what? Why would anyone want that kind of trouble? At the same time, several public right-to-know cases had been won and there was ample evidence of military re-supplying of war hardware to all of the major law enforcement agencies in the nation. Suddenly, local cops had armor, assault weapons and heavy artillery. In the bigger cities, they had been sold assault choppers and had non-lethal helicopters retrofitted with heavy guns.

The idea that America was going to be invaded was a pipe dream of war hawks and bait for fools. It was more likely that these armaments were going to be used to quell domestic insurgencies.

There was a piece to this puzzle missing, he thought. Why stir up trouble just to put it down and really, if all of the people were to rise up, there wasn't enough firepower to stop it. The operation had to be a specific, almost surgical strike and the places where the current riots were happening didn't seem to be in centers of influence.

If there was a plot, no matter how remote, Meyerson's 9-11 evidence would be a significant hindrance. The story was so explosive, that people would question everything their government was doing. Indeed, if there was a shadow organization, all of government would come into question.

Detroit was no exception to the trends he saw. The city had just had another national police involved murder of a black girl, killed in a police station no less.

The case had been solved but it only added to the public's suspicion of law enforcement and the widening gulf between blacks and whites.

They crossed the Detroit Grosse Pointe border. Once inside the city, they would find a base and then use local transit. Detroit was still behind the times and most city busses were not equipped with CCTV.

Luther did recall that the FBI and Homeland had recently used a new technology for monitoring urban populations. It was illegal and blew up in their faces when it inadvertently recorded a murder.

"I didn't get that business on the boat at first," said Meyerson. "Then I put it together. That guy, in Canada split the take but probably took most of it and so the transport guys were going to ask us for money on the other side. You countered with a robbery to stop them and cover our true purpose."

"Long way to go but yes," said Luther.

"Normally, I'm quicker but I am getting old."

"So is that how perfect memory works?" asked Luther. "Information overload?"

"No," said Meyerson. "It's actually like a big warehouse with all these little colored marbles. When the colors pile up, you know something is about to happen. Like since we've been walking, I've been noticing the traffic lights and the flow of cars, civilian, city, and the like. So according to what I know, a police cruiser is about to pass us on the cross street down there."

Luther looked ahead but saw only normal cars, then suddenly a police cruiser passed them from behind. It stopped at a light then slowed as two young black men crossed the intersection.

"Right call, wrong street," said Luther.

Suddenly, the two young men took off running. The police cruiser hit its siren and gave pursuit.

"Welcome to Detroit," said Luther.

They went to a bus stop and waited. A homeless man slept behind the bench on the ground. Wrapped in covers, he looked like someone's discarded trash.

The plan was simple, they would get the information, extract it, then Luther would take it to the agency and let them sort it out.

Of course, if Meyerson and Bane were telling the truth, there was a chance the Core would kill him before he could accomplish this. If there was a Core, then they'd have agents on the case by now. It would only take one to pull a trigger.

"We could just drop all this," said Meyerson. "I mean; what difference does it make who runs America? The people are still gonna get it up the ass no matter what."

"Makes a difference to me," said Luther. "When there is no right and wrong, then everything is wrong."

"Boy, was she right about you."

"If I wasn't that kind of guy, you'd be dead."

They took the first bus that came by. It was an older model and there were only a few riders. Luther and Meyerson sat in the same row but on opposite sides of the aisle.

They were moving west toward their destination. As they went further into the city proper, Luther saw the familiar creep of decay, only this time it was resisted by new areas of development. The occasional new building and commercial oasis popped up and that gave him some hope for the city.

The bus stopped and a young black man got on. He paid his toll and then surveyed the people on the bus. There was only Luther, Meyerson and an old woman who sat all the way in the rear.

The young black man was wearing the standard ghetto wannabe tough uniform. Sagging jeans, sports jersey, lots of fake bling. He passed by Luther and Meyerson and sat near the back.

The old lady got off at the next stop and the young black man moved back their way and sat behind Meyerson.

"Where you headed, pops?" he asked.

Meyerson said nothing. The young man was about to say something else when Luther attacked.

Luther shot up onto his feet, set himself and punched the young man hard in the jaw. He finished with a hook and knocked him out cold.

Luther pushed him to the side of the seat as the bus driver looked back to see what the commotion was about. All he saw was three passengers, one of whom was asleep. He kept driving.

"What was that?" asked Meyerson.

"We have to move," said Luther.

Luther took a gun, a serrated knife and money from the young man and then pulled the stop cord. The driver pulled over then he and Meyerson exited.

On the street, Luther immediately walked toward a residential area.

"First car we see, we buy a ride," said Luther.

"That kid was going to rob me?" asked Meyerson.

"Maybe," said Luther. "He was going to antagonize you first. No need to wait for that to play out. I knew where it was going. We logged a few miles on the bus. As we get further in, it gets more dangerous."

They walked the streets until Luther saw an elderly man named Hickey.

Hickey had an old vintage silver 1980 Cadillac and was very proud of it.

Luther chatted him up then paid him from the money he'd just lifted and they were driven toward their destination.

Hickey barely looked at the funds. Luther guessed he was a retiree and just liked the company that came with giving rides.

They got into the backseat of the spacious car. It smelled of cheap incense and the seats were made of a lurid orange velvet.

"This is a 1980," said Hickey. "These seats is custom, crushed velvet. Only made fifty of these bad boys. I got one because I used to Works for GM back in the day. I started as a welder but in the end, I was in quality control. That A-Plan will put you in any Hog you want."

Meyerson looked at Luther quizzically.

"A Hog is slang for a Cadillac," said Luther.

"That's right," said Hickey. "Cause this bad boy hogs the road when you drive it."

Al Green played on the stereo. Why did these old heads all love Al Green? Luther thought. Must be something about his songs that made them feel nostalgic.

His father was an Al Green fan, Luther thought. It would be nice to see his family while he was here but he knew better. No need to cause more trouble. No, he'd finish this and then leave quietly and let his people think he was still safe abroad.

"V-8 engine," Hickey continued. "Big one. Two hunnet horsepower." He hit the gas and the car lurched. "Course, she ain't what he used to be. Where you boys headed?"

Meyerson directed him and as they came closer, the city reshaped itself again. Now in its heart of darkness, the streets were filled with the underclass, although many streets looked uninhabited.

"You probably don't believe this, but I'm a Republican," said Hickey. "I did vote for Obama but that was history. Otherwise, I think we all need to get back to Jesus, you know. Take this gay marriage thing." Hickey hesitated. "You boys ain't gay are you?"

Luther and Meyerson both laughed and then answered that they were not.

"Good," said Meyerson. "I'm not a hateful man. I love everybody but this gay marriage thing is crazy. It says it right there in the bible— no fags. And still here they come, wanting to be like regular folks. No sir, if they want to get hooked up, they need to call it by another name, a non-biblical name. Call it ass union, butt bonding or something."

Meyerson was chuckling and Luther did not try to discourage him. He didn't want to engage the man in a debate. Really, he didn't care about marriage laws. They were only there to make people feel secure. The only reason for marriage was to control wealth and lineage. Everything else was bullshit.

"And look at the kids now," Hickey continued. "The girls all dress like hoes and the boys too, walking around with their asses showing. No respect. Just last week, I had one of them knuckleheads try me. But I got me a fo-five right here under my seat. I won't take it out. Don't wanna scare you boys. I did a little stint in the military and I've always been handy with a gun."

"A little stint?" asked Meyerson.

"Well, you know, I had a problem with authority," said Hickey. "Kept telling my sergeant to suck my dick. She didn't appreciate that."

Hickey was not a big man, Luther thought. A .45 was a pretty big gun for a frail man like him.

"Anyway, the fool sees that gun and he 'bout pissed his pants. And I said, 'when you see this caddy, you just turn and run the next time, or I will put a hot one in your little monkey ass.' Well, he ran like he was in the damned NFL or something, just disappeared."

Hickey continued to talk in his colorful way as they moved further inside the city's neighborhoods. He'd wave to a person every once in a while and even stopped to flirt with a woman walking home from a grocery store.

Luther could barely remember guys like Hickey growing up. He had been such a serious kid. He loved his books and study, sports teams and later, the R.O.T.C. which was the start of everything for him.

Meyerson instructed Hickey to let them off on a desolate looking corner near Eight Mile.

They got out and thanked Hickey who was all too happy to take them back to wherever they'd come from. Luther politely refused and he and Meyerson walked down the street then cut over.

"What are we looking for?" asked Meyerson.

"A safehouse," said Luther. "A motel with one visible access."

They walked for several miles, before settling on a little motel called The Palm on the city's northern border at Eight Mile. The Palm was a good location for them to hold up because of its configuration.

Meyerson had wondered why Luther shunned the other motels whose faces where close to or flush with the street. These places offered little room in which to place surveillance and counter measures.

In the urban field, an agent always had to secure his safehouse by making sure he has not been tracked or discovered.

The Palm sat in from the street separated by a big parking lot and the business office. There was no access to it from the back, which meant there was only one way to approach.

It also had a flag pole on one end and a telephone pole line on the other, perfect places to put cameras to sweep the general area, which is just what he did.

The feeds from the cameras transmitted to a server which he could access anywhere. Luther always took his gear with him. You never left anything at a safehouse when you were in the urban field. You never knew if you'd be going back.

Luther searched the local news and found the story on the discovery of Cantini's body. A man they called The Farmer had come into that neighborhood and wanted to plant a garden on the land. The place was overrun with drug activity but this guy, who was apparently a vet, had cleared them out in a manner of weeks.

The article showed the man with a .44 magnum on his hip holding a machete.

When this Farmer had begun work, he found a body in a shallow grave. He had called a detective friend of his and the police had come and removed the body and made the lot a crime scene, which meant the farm had to wait.

The remains of the man were skeletal and wrapped in decaying plastic. But the important part of the story was that the body had one of the first new-gen prosthetic limbs, a Poesner LH-7 titanium leg.

This had made it easier to ID the corpse, Robert Cantini, who had gone missing along with his wife and daughter on the night of September 10, 2001.

Eventually, the wife and daughter were found in another grave in the yard of a neighbor not far from their home.

"A brutal night," said Luther.

"High stakes," said Meyerson.

Luther went back to the story on Cantini. He and his family were all interred in a graveyard in the city. Cantini had received a military burial.

"They're not buried," said Luther. "They're in a family mausoleum."

"Yes, but it's a ways from here. So, we rob the grave?" asked Meyerson.

"Yes," said Luther. "That's exactly what we're gonna do."

12

Clean

Clement drove toward his warehouse. It was just a couple of miles from his place of business in a little industrial park that had been abandoned by Coca Cola some years ago.

There were three tenants in Powell Complex now, Clement, a storage facility called U Keep It and a Ford consumer testing facility.

Clement liked having this place away from the business, made him feel like a mogul. It wasn't very big but it was all his and he limited access very strictly. Trent had a code but he had to tell Clement whenever he went and keep a log of visits.

Clement also had cameras all over that he turned off whenever he was there but for others, it recorded everything they did.

He kept a little office in the rear and it was equipped with a shower and a bed. He sometimes slept there overnight.

Trent never complained but he didn't like it. He thought Clement was stepping out on him with hot young guys or maybe women. When they'd met, Trent didn't believe Clement was gay.

Clement hated that term. He did not think of himself as gay or worse, homosexual. He was a man who preferred sex with men. He didn't dislike women, he just didn't feel a spark with them. Also, most of them he found annoying, vain and troublesome.

When Clement read all the controversy about gays in the news, he just laughed. It was all so damned silly. People wouldn't know how to behave without their prejudices.

The only person who really understood him was his sister. She was a teacher and married to a good guy

named Dennis Cole. He sent them money every month
and told Dennis that it was her percentage of their
business. It was a lie but he didn't want Dennis to think
that he was getting a handout. A man had to feel a
sense of pride and independence.

Also, he wanted him to view his sister as valuable.
He really hoped he didn't have to kill Dennis one day.

They had two kids, a girl named Melissa and a boy
named Mertren, named for Dennis' grandfather. They
called him Mert. The girl was typical kid but Mert was
special. He was a handful. Just six years old and he was
already tagged as a bad kid at his school.

Clement could sense the danger and menace in the
kid. When the time came, he and Mert would become
close and he'd show the kid that he was not the odd
one, everyone else was.

Clement pulled up to the warehouse and walked to
the safety door. He dialed his security system on his
cell and spoke into the phone, saying his name, then a
code which opened the big steel door and turned off
the surveillance system.

Clement entered and took in a deep breath as the
door closed behind him. He loved the earthy and
chemical smells of the warehouse.

He could tell what each crate or vat held without
looking. A sharp, acrid smell hit him as he moved
through. There was death in these containers, endless
possibilities.

He'd received another message from Red Dogg,
giving him the general area to look for his targets. How
they were tracking them was a mystery but something
he did not care to know. He had learned long ago not
to become too curious about how the higher ups did
business. It was not healthy.

He was giddy at the prospect of eliminating two
dangerous men. When he was done, he might even
skip killing for a year, maybe take a vacation with
Trent. That would be nice.

The last true adversary he had, happened by
accident. Clement loved to relive his kills in his head.
But each time, the memories satisfied him less and less
which is why he always needed new ones. But this one
always made him happy. It was one of his favorites.

He'd gone into the city on a Friday night in the
summer and encountered a band of drug dealers. Their
leader was a rather sickly looking man named Cuzzin,
who nonetheless was feared in the neighborhood.

Cuzzin was a tall, sinewy man with a shaved head
and yellow, watery eyes. He was about twenty-eight or
so. Pretty old for the drug game. Usually, by that age,
they were dead, in prison or broken into so many
pathetic pieces. But not Cuzzin. He was smart and
mean, a man who knew how to stay out of harm's way.

Clement had watched and tracked the man for most
of the night. Cuzzin moved around boldly, striking fear
wherever he went.

Clement had camped out near a drug den and
watched Cuzzin in action as he had to discipline some
of his workers. He had cursed the boys, humiliated
them and then beaten them severely with this bare
hands.

Clement was tingly with the prospect of killing this
man. He was evil, ruthless and could handle himself.
Of course, it was easy to beat up two unarmed kids.
When he got Cuzzin, it would be a real contest.

Cuzzin left with his bodyguard at his side. He made
several other stops, making sure his business was
running well and no one had shorted his take.

He went to what had to be his home base, a very
nice little house in one of the better neighborhoods.
Here, he did not keep a high profile. There were no
guards, nothing that indicated his occupation.

Clement sneaked into the home easily but Cuzzin
had somehow been alerted. He was waiting for
Clement as he emerged from the rear of the place.

The dealer open fire on Clement with an auto pistol which had almost caught him.

"You dead, bitch!" Cuzzin had yelled.

An auto gun had a kick and it threw your aim off. Their utility was they spewed a lot of bullets. Unfortunately, it decreased your change of hitting what you were aiming at.

"You got no idea who you fucking wif, nigga!"

But thanks to Cuzzin's big mouth, Clement did have an idea where Cuzzin's position was.

Clement maneuvered away but Cuzzin was moving in on him. The dealer kept shooting, then suddenly his gun dry clicked. The clip had not been full.

Cuzzin scrambled for a fresh clip from his pants. Clement understood that if he reloaded the gun, he would be dead in a second round of shooting.

Clement pulled a taser he had constructed for long-rage use. It sailed across the room and caught Cuzzin in the meaty part of his thigh from the rear.

The drug dealer went down immediately, dropping the clip and the gun before he could reload. His body shook and shimmied as he pissed his pants.

The common misconception about tasers is that voltage equals strength. This is not true. Amperage is where the power is. A heart defibrillator delivers about one or two amps. Clement's taser was twice that, like being hit by lightning.

Clement robbed Cuzzin of his money and gaudy jewelry to make it look like a robbery and then he had cut him up and deposited him into the foundation of what was now a Taco Bell.

Coming out of his memory, Clement stopped at a fenced off area in the warehouse. The very corrosive compounds had to be kept here by law. He opened the little gate and removed a small barrel of concentrated sulfuric. There were normally special rules for transporting these but he wasn't going on an official job.

He loaded the barrel into his little SUV and secured it in the rear. He then headed toward the city's eastern border. Red Dogg had given him a pretty big area to cover.

He'd searched for the better part of a day but had no luck. The pictures of the two men were not very good and many people looked alike to him, especially the black ones.

Red Dogg had given him another updated tracking. This time, Clement got lucky and caught sight of two men fitting the description going into a sleazy motel which sat at the back of a big lot.

He saw them leave but he did not follow. He knew they would be back as they had not checked out. The black one was big and looked in great shape. Clement would take him first, he thought. But first he had to get rid of the motel's employee.

Clement casually walked up to The Palm and went inside. The clerk was a thin man with a long face and scraggly beard. He wore a Green Lantern t-shirt.

"Help you?" asked the clerk.

Clement barely heard this as he was looking for the motel's camera system. He found it in the back right corner. The light on the tiny camera was flashing and so it was recording.

"Yes," said Clement and then he pulled his taser and shot him in the chest.

The clerk went stiff and Clement heard gas escape him as he fell hard on the floor.

Clement went to him as his body still twitched and bound and gagged him securely. Clement suffocated him and then packed him into a little utility room and sealed the door.

He got the security tape, erased it and then he shut off the system all together.

Clement then went back to the desk and checked the registry. There were six guests and none of the names looked legit to him.

The clerk he'd just killed was named George Madijhian.

George kept a record of all the people who checked in. No one gave a real name in a place like this, so George probably just wanted to make sure he knew who they were to him in case the police came asking questions.

Five of the six tenants were male-female couples. Only one were two men located in room six. George had written *"Don't seem gay but you can never tell these days."*

These were his guys, Clement thought.

He left the office with a broom and dust pan and pretended to clean up the area. A man came out of a unit and got into a car and drove off. The door to the room was open and Clement saw a woman inside wearing only panties. She looked after the man then closed the door.

He fake-cleaned his way around the area, getting a feel for the place. He saw room six but did not go to it. He'd wait for them to return, then get a confirm to go from Red Dogg. If it checked out, he'd gas them in their sleep and then the fun would begin.

13

The Palm

The Cantini mausoleum had a prominent place in Woodmere Cemetery where many historic figures were buried. Luther wondered how a government worker was able to afford such an expensive resting place. But a quick check of the family lineage answered this. Apparently, one side of the family was legit and the other had accumulated a fortune from old criminal ties.

Luther and Meyerson easily walked onto the grounds. No one liked to mess around in a graveyard so there was little security. Woodmere no longer had a groundskeeper but a company that did occasional drive-by checks.

Luther and Meyerson removed the heavy door and let the interior air out. Often gasses got trapped inside and if you weren't careful, you could get overwhelmed.

Luther was surprised to find only one coffin inside, a huge box that looked like it had been made from two smaller ones. It didn't take long for him to conclude that all three family members were inside.

Luther pried the lid open and found the remains of the Cantini family. He quickly searched the man's body, pulling his knife in case he had to sever a harness.

Luther felt the left leg and there it was, the prosthetic. It looked bulky but it had set the new standard for what military men got when they lost a limb today.

"Got it," said Luther easily pulling it off. "We're lucky. Whoever laid these people to rest took their valuables. Look at the bodies, he has no tie on and it looks like a necklace was pulled off the wife and tossed back. It's rusted, so they realized it was not gold."

"Goddamned grave-robbers," Meyerson mumbled.

"No, just poor people," said Luther. "Thank goodness they were too superstitious to take the leg. This thing is actually worth something."

Meyerson held a light as Luther extracted a small cylinder near the knee joint. Luther recognized the old data reserve units, or DRU, which eventually became thumb drives. This one was housed in steel and bore a designation number.

Luther and Meyerson closed the coffin on the Cantini family. The heavy door didn't quite fit as it should have but there was no time to be neat about it. That roving security guard might come by and then, they'd have trouble.

They made their way back across the city, walking, taking the bus and buying rides. They stayed away from *Uber* and *Lyft* drivers as you needed to give them too much information to ride.

They stopped at a fast food chain called Olga's and ate. Luther did not care much for fast food but this place made a very tasty Greek-style bread he enjoyed.

"You no longer have to stay with this," said Luther.

"After I see what's on that drive," said Meyerson.

"I thought you put this together," said Luther a little surprised.

"I did," said Meyerson. "And of course, I remember what's on it but some of the information was put on by my friend and I never saw that. My info was very suspicious but he had much more."

"Fair enough," said Luther. He was thinking that if anything happened to him, that Meyerson's brain would always have a copy of the evidence.

"In case you are wondering," said Meyerson. "My funds have not been frozen. I will have plenty of money to get away."

"Because they are waiting for you to access them," said Luther." And when you do, they have you."

"Not if I do it correctly," said Meyerson.

Luther pulled out his computer and called up the footage from The Palm. He scrolled through it, watching carefully.

"Looks good," said Luther. "Very little activity since we've been gone."

Meyerson looked at the footage. Luther did not care this as Meyerson had that steel trap mind.

"Anything?" Luther asked.

"No," said Meyerson. "The shift change came for the night man. Other than that, there's just the normal stuff."

"Then let's go," said Luther. "I don't want to access the info here in public and the motel has a strong Internet connection."

They made their way back to the motel and though they were sure the place was clean, they still staggered their entrance, Meyerson going in first and then Luther five minutes later.

Inside, Luther quickly connected to the E-1 server and accessed the DRU drive. The information was encrypted and so it took a while.

"Here it comes," said Luther as the first files loaded.

There were document memos from people in the Pentagon and the CIA. As they loaded, Luther noticed there were no communications from the White House and only one from a U.S. Senator who was now deceased.

The video Meyerson had referred to was a meeting between two men and a woman who talked openly about the coming assault.

"That's General Davenport, Bob Lefts from the agency and Alicia Ford, she's a Server, like me," said Meyerson.

"Davenport and Lefts are both dead," said Luther. "Davenport had cancer and Lefts had a skiing accident, or that's what was reported at the time."

"Alicia is dead too," said Meyerson. "It didn't make the papers but she disappeared on a commute in 2004

at a gas station and they never found her. I remember
that the gas station's cameras were off right at the time
she was there. That meant she was taken or she ran."

"They cleaned house," said Luther. He clicked on the
video and it began to play:

"When will the planes hit?" asked Davenport.
"Morning, that's much as we know," said Lefts.
"Information is limited for obvious reasons."
"This had better work," said Ford. "The media will be all
over this. This fucking Internet thing is like goddamned Big
Brother."
"And we're sure the buildings will fall?" asked
Davenport. "It's essential that they do."
"Again General," said Lefts. "We can only speculate. Our
operatives have worked independently such that each team
thinks they are the only one working. We have three
components and they have all reported positively to us
through channels."
"I get the concern, Bob," said Ford. "And what about the
fallout? I mean, the area is going to be uninhabitable for a
while, isn't it?"
"Wer're counting on that," said Lefts. "This will give us
time to erase all doubt, put in our counter informational
measures and generally get the public off on their usual
tangents about race and terrorism."
"And the informational concern?" asked Davenport. "Did
we clean up all the communications that might be
damning?"
"Yes," said Lefts. "We had funding for a system overhaul
come through congress last year and we used it to delete
thousands of files even if they might suggest knowledge of
this."
"And what about Meyerson?" asked Davenport. "Did we
resolve that?"
"He wouldn't come in," said Ford. "I did what I could."
"He's going to be taking a meeting there in tower one
when it happens," said Lefts.

They all laughed, and it was evil, nervous laughter.
"Okay then," said Davenport. "Our people are ready to move, so hold on to your asses."

"Who took the video?" said Luther.
"You'll see," said Meyerson.
The three on the video left and the camera showed nothing for over an hour. Thang, a man entered and took the camera out. Luther briefly saw his face as he looked into the lens and said:
"Sorry, pal. But at least now you know."
"That's Jennings," said Meyerson. "He's the guy that tipped me."
"Here's the new info," said Luther.
He pulled up articles and internal memos from three lobbying firms in Washington D.C.: Kilt and Associates. Spector, Danker & Travers and a firm called Vantage. There were hundreds of men and women working at the three firms but the papers began to narrow it down to about twenty or so men and women who were the Core.
"Henry Kilt, Greg Spector and Rylan Trot," said Luther. "That's about half a trillion dollars right there."
"There are probably ten or twelve others associated with them but this seems to be the brain and money trust."
"Look here," said Luther. "Projection on their net worth just from arms and fuel sales. They've moved in on everything, food, clean water, lithium and land acquisitions."
"Lithium?" asked Meyerson.
"Green tech," said Luther. Batteries for cars.
"Jesus, Afghanistan," said Meyerson. "I forgot."
Afghanistan had one of the richest deposits of lithium in the world. There was so much talk about oil, that no one in the media ever talked about this fact but the government knew and that had made the country a target.

"They've also put a lot of money into lobbying for trade agreements," said Luther.

The last file loaded. Luther opened it and though he had seen many terrible things in his day, he was still shocked by the headline:

TACTICAL URBAN ASSAULT PLAN,
MIGRATION PROJECTIONS,
ESTABLISHMENT CLAUSE DECONSTRUCTION.

"What the fuck is this?" asked Luther to himself. "This is part of something else. Looks like these people were looking at a long term op."

"Every country has an urban assault plan," said Meyerson casually. "It's always where the trouble starts."

"But why the need to track the migration of people? And this doesn't track them by race but by religious affiliation and class. And this last one is part of a plan to attack the Establishment Clause."

"And do what, have a United States Church of America?"

"England had a church and many countries do," said Luther. "But what's the end game of all this? Disrupt the cities, force dissension on religion? Why?"

"Money," said Meyerson. "It's always money in the end."

"Money is a given," said Luther. "Something bigger has to be the goal. Look, this was fifteen years ago. By now, there has to be a more comprehensive plan. I've got to go to D.C."

"It's too big," said Meyerson. "If they've been working on it for this long, then the wheels are already turning."

"But a long term operation doesn't have a time table," said Luther. "What it does have is an inciting event. Look here under urban assault, there are multiple references to Chicago. Lots of people dying there in the last few years."

"What does that do?" asked Meyerson, a little concern in his voice.

"Could be several things," said Luther. "Could just be coincidence. But for the sake of argument, let's say it's to lead the nation into thinking of the city as a violent place where bad things happen."

"The city's mayor was a D.C. insider not too long ago," said Meyerson.

"That could be coincidental, too," said Luther. "But at this point, I count nothing out."

"Shit!" said Meyerson suddenly.

"What is it?" asked Luther urgently.

"The surveillance video on the Palm. A man went into the business office on that shift change but the other guy didn't come out!"

It took Luther a few seconds to put it together. If a shift change happened, why didn't the relieved clerk come out of the office? Luther packed his gear and pulled his weapon.

"Our seal was still on the door, so he hasn't been in here," said Luther. "We have to go."

"Can't believe I missed that," said Meyerson.

"No time for that," said Luther. "We leave just to make sure you're not seeing things."

Luther opened the little closet and Meyerson heard a crash as Luther kicked down the flimsy wall between their unit and the one next door. That unit was on a corner.

Meyerson followed Luther inside and they emerged in the room next to theirs, which was empty. From there, they went into the bathroom and out a back window.

"Why didn't he try to take us?" asked Meyerson.

"If there's a guy," said Luther. "He's waiting for night," said Luther. "He's not from E-1. An E-1 agent would have just attacked as soon as he had a shot."

Luther squeezed through the bathroom window after taking off the grate. Outside, the back of the unit was a few feet in front of a wall. He had to slip down and move sideways but soon they were headed toward a field which abutted the motel and was filled with power limes.

In the field, they could see the parking lot and the business office. Luther checked his weapon.

"How did they track us?" asked Meyerson. "Wer've been very— "

Before he could finish, Luther took out a scanner, turned it on and began to run it over Meyerson.

"Bane was the only one alone with you for any time before me," said Luther. "I was so worried about her complicity and then eliminating her that I— "

The scanner chirped as Luther ran it by Meyerson's right calf. Luther rolled up his pant leg and saw a small bump in the back of his calf.

Meyerson winced as Luther took out a knife and cut the RFD chip out. Luther smashed it, cursing as he did.

"Mini RFD," said Luther. "Small but it sends a pulse every few hours or so. Wide-ranging but you can narrow it down by elimination."

Meyerson was wiping the blood from his leg. "So, we run now," he said.

"You go," said Luther. "I need to take that man out. I can't be looking over my shoulder while I finish this."

"No, I stay until the end, then I go," said Meyerson. His sincerity was genuine. Luther was not surprised by this. He expected Meyerson's sense of duty to kick in at some point.

"You stay outside of the office and just watch for locals and take this," said Luther handing him the gun he'd lifted from the man on the bus.

They moved toward the business office. Luther got himself ready. He now had the element of surprise. And if there was a killer on their trail, he'd only have one chance to get him.

****

When it became dark, Clement would go to unit six, drop a knockout bomb into it and extract the men.

They did not look particularly lethal to him when they'd returned. The black one was big but he'd taken out guys even bigger than him in the city.

Clement was going to dissolve one of them and the other he'd drop in pieces along the train tracks leading out of the city. There were three cargo trains headed out tomorrow and so the tracks would be the perfect place to put the parts and let the train pulverize them. He'd watch of course, because that was the best part.

Suddenly, he heard a car pull up. In the parking lot, a blue Toyota angled into a slot and a man came in. He was white and middle aged. He had that 'just picked up a hooker' look of nervousness on his face. Clement glanced at the car. The woman inside was young but hardly a hooker. Office romance, he thought absently.

"Need a room," said the man.

"No problema," said Clement.

"Where's Victor?" asked the man. "He usually… forget it."

"If you had an arrangement with Vic," said Clement, "I'd be happy to honor it but he didn't leave instructions."

"I take room three there and I just leave the money, no register."

"Fine by me," said Clement. "I'll just tell him when he comes back. He's under the weather."

The man left some bills and Clement took them and gave him a keycard for room three. The man hurried back to his car and drove away.

When Clement turned his attentions back to his surveillance, he felt a presence to his right. In the instant, he thought it was clever to sneak up on him while he was occupied. But how did his marks know?

He turned, raising his arm to block an assault. With the other, he pulled his weapon.

****

Meyerson's head was buzzing. Something was not right but he could not put it together. This damned thing was a curse sometimes.

He knew that he'd had granola for breakfast on a Monday, June 5, 1989 but he could not say why he suddenly felt nervous.

When he got out of this, he was going to collect Joust and move to New Zealand. That had really been his first choice but it made it harder to keep track of his family.

He should have known that they would never let him go with what he knew. Powerful men never let people go. They just found new ways to kill them—

That was it, he thought as the information suddenly formed and rushed by his mind's eye. This had all been too easy. Why would anyone want to kill them *before* they got the information? He bolted towards the office.

****

Luther threw a punch that was blocked by the man at the clerk's desk. The man countered, swinging a weapon up.

Luther deflected the blow, sending the Taser's projectiles into the ceiling.

Luther caught him in the midsection with a front kick before the man could retract the projectiles and try again.

The man took the blow and used the force to roll away but Luther followed his own momentum, which gave the man no time to recover.

The man turned and his face showed surprise to find Luther within attack distance. He obviously did not know what he was up against and was used to lesser opponents.

The man attacked nonetheless and Luther could tell he had some training. The punches had force and were angled precisely.

Luther easily countered his attacks, slipping punches and maneuvering him into a tighter space. He could see panic rise in the man's eyes.

Luther allowed the man to strike a glancing blow and used the man's angle to strike his own blow to the man's kidneys which hobbled him. Luther straightened him with a knee to the chin then smashed his nose with a flat palm blow.

The man was strong but no match for Luther who soon had him wobbly, then dropped him with a short hook to the side of the head.

The duo battled close to the office's window. Luther now stood to one side of it, never thinking about it.

Meyerson rushed in and Luther jerked around to see him, pulling away from the open window.

"Set up!" yelled Meyerson.

Luther dropped to the floor as the office window exploded.

Meyerson was hit in the head. The force of it twisted him around so that the second bullet actually hit him in the back of the head.

The whole thing was a decoy, Luther thought. This would-be assassin was some low level clean up man who had been duped to lure Luther out, while the real assassin followed and waited to kill them all.

Luther crawled to Meyerson. He was dead. Luther took his gear. He would need Meyerson's accounts and any contacts he had.

"...five, six, seven, eight..." Luther counted as he scrambled toward the back.

He was counting how long before the shooter realized he would not get another shot and had to erase the target with more firepower. There was no more reason for subtlety. The killer had to backwash them all. That's what he would do.

Luther slipped out the back of the office building, quickly got to his feet, then sprinted to the wall at the rear of the place.

All the while he was still counting. By now, the killer had pulled his second weapon, sighted a target and informed his handlers what he was going to do.

It was a masterful plan and it might have worked if Meyerson was not so clever. He had saved Luther's life and in the process lost his own.

Luther heard the high sharp whistle of the mini rocket as it sailed across Eight Mile and hit the little business office at The Palm, blowing it into a million pieces.

The force of the explosion pushed him forward. He rolled, got up and kept moving. He jumped over a wall and began to move away as fast as he could. The height of the wall shielded him from the sniper but still he kept as low as he could.

Luther got into a rhythm as he put distance between himself and the explosion. He turned onto a residential street, targeted the oldest car on the block and stole it. In the chaos of the explosion and fire, no one would be looking for this vehicle.

He had to get out of Detroit and soon. There were deadly men involved in this operation and he now had vital information. Which meant he had a new mission. No manner of reason or politics would help in this fight. These were men of means, power and will. He had to change the game.

He had to kill them all.

****

Across the wide boulevard from the Palm, a van sat on the top of a small office parking structure, a panel had been cut and was open.

In the back, the assassin cursed and rose from a shooting position, then sent word that only one of the targets had been eliminated.

"Unfortunate," said a voice on a radio.

"I'll get him," said Sharon Bane. "He can only kill me once."

14

Ghost

Grosse Isle, Michigan.
Las Vegas, Nevada.

Luther drove his first stolen car into Southgate, where he dumped it, then procured another. From there, he moved downriver towards Grosse Isle Airport.

He had a plan but it was very dangerous. His pursuers would expect him to hit the interstate and that's where they'd be looking. The airports were tricky but only if he flew out of the big ones.

Luther broke into a business office in Novi and used their computer lines to access his E-1 backdoor. He then hacked the Air Marshall database and registered himself under the name David Henderson. He changed clothes, dressing in the intentionally inconspicuous clothing of an Air Marshall. He also changed his look, adding a beard and changing his jawline.

He then rented a car under the new identity, paying with an unregistered debit card. Luther then drove the rented vehicle the rest of the way to the little airport and went to security.

He registered as an Air Marshall and waited for his confirmation. The security and TSA people checked his weapons and he let them, signing in for their register and even taking a photo.

Luther hung with the security team after his confirmation came back and they warmed up to him. He talked sports, saying he played college ball but got injured and made up a stint in the U.S. Army.

It was all going smoothly, until the head of Grosse Isle airport security came in.

Frank V. Lambert was an old school FBI agent and well into his sixties. He was a conservative and was one of those bosses who ran a tight ship.

Luther had researched him of course and he was as clean as they came: military, police detective, then FBI service rising to regional manager, then retirement. Married once for forty years, father of three, grandfather of five, registered Republican.

Lambert entered the waiting room and when he did, Luther stood and greeted him. He was surprised when the other men and women did the same.

"Sir," said Luther.

"Don't get a lot of Air Marshals here," said Lambert, getting right to the point. "I just stopped in to get something and I heard. We got trouble?"

Lambert was casual and folksy but Luther could see the calculation behind it all. This was not only a good agent, he was wise, which was much more dangerous.

"No sir," said Luther. "But if there was, I wouldn't be able to speak on it, sir."

"Military?" asked Lambert

"Yes sir. Sorry, old habits."

"Where did you serve?" Thé interrogation continue.

"Two tours in Iraq. I did long recon with the 27th."

"Dangerous work," said Lambert looking impressed.

"Yes, but blessedly uneventful. We were fired upon but none of my band ever got hit."

"Have a seat," said Lambert.

Luther did and Lambert sat across from him. He eyed Luther suspiciously and it was clear that something had set him off. Luther thought hard, trying to get ahead of whatever it was.

"I've requested Marshals before," said Lambert. "Don't know why they wouldn't tell me first."

"I was activated just this evening," said Luther. "If you'd like, I could call Fetty and ask but you know how he is."

Ralph Jettison was the regional Marshall contact out of Metro in Detroit. Luther had checked on him as well and he was known to be an asshole.

"Yes, I do," said Lambert. "No need, I guess."

"Doesn't make any sense to me," said Luther. "Everyone knows GIA has a perfect security score. I thought I'd be going out of Grand Rapids or worse, Saginaw."

Lambert laughed a little. Those other airports had much lower ratings and Luther had known this as well.

"Can't be number one without a little flack, I guess," said Lambert.

"No sir, I wouldn't think so. I just go where they tell me."

"Interesting sidearm," said Lambert. "Fancy gun. I'm a Smith and Wesson man myself."

Now he was testing his knowledge of guns. Luther almost wanted to laugh at this.

"I carried Glock for years," said Luther. "Hated them. The Walther is very reliable and it packs a punch. Had to get special permission though. You know the government."

"You mind?" asked Lambert.

"No sir," said Luther.

He took his P99 and removed the clip and the round in the chamber then presented it to Lambert like they were taught in the military.

Lambert took it, felt it out, looked down the sight.

"A beauty," said Lambert as he handed it back. "Where you headed."

"Toledo, then I don't know. Can't imagine that will be my last stop."

"Well, it was great to meet you," said Lambert. "What city you live in?"

"Detroit," said Luther. "Far eastside."

"Well, if you ever want to work here, call us. We're always looking for good men."

"I will certainly keep that in mind," said Luther. "But the Marshal Service has been pretty good to me."

Lambert left and when he did, the other security people breathed easier. Lambert was a task master and none of them said a word while he was there.

They all seemed to be impressed that Luther was able to handle him. They had no way of knowing that each response was tailored to disarm the old man. All of Luther's responses cut just under the accomplishments of Lambert who was an Alpha type and would be inclined to harass a man who was too weak or too strong.

Soon, Luther was aboard a little jumper to Toledo International. From there, he flew to small airports in Kentucky, then Colorado and into Nevada.

He was allowed on all flights without payment. The staff all kissed his ass profusely. He got the phone number of one flight attendant and best of all, he got to fly with his weapons.

Once in Las Vegas, he reached out to Alex and had gotten an immediate response. It had been a very exhausting twenty-four hours and now Luther was sitting in a strip club with his old friend watching Alex's girlfriend perform.

Alex Deavers had changed since Luther last saw him at the Lincoln Memorial in Washington. He had indeed repaired his face but he would never be the handsome Alex of old. He still had scarring on one side of his face like a very subtle Two-Face from *Batman*.

And Alex had bulked up, putting on at least ten pounds of muscle which he attributed to HGH and Testosterone injections.

"I got really sick," said Deavers. "My immune system was weak. The docs put me on this program and now I look like The Rock."

"Not quite like that," said Luther.

"So, here you are in the hot-seat again," said Alex.

"Not by my choosing."

"Chicago," said Alex. "I wondered why the bodies were piling up. They're saying it's gangs, the economy but killing like that is classic pre-operational. Makes sense though."

"How so?" asked Luther.

"I keep forgetting you haven't been in the U.S.," said Alex. "Chicago's hosting an event called The Holy Rebels to protest police shootings, banks, climate change, all the current trendy anti-establishment causes. It mostly faith-based organizations from all over the nation."

"Where and how many?" asked Luther.

"Lakefront. It's going to be televised and they are expecting thirty thousand over two days.'

"That's got to be it," said Luther. "Something's going to happen there an assassination or…"

Luther grew quiet. If the new plan was as big as he thought, then it needed an inciting event even bigger than the last one, something while maybe not as spectacular, certainly more evil.

"Blow it all up, kill them all," said Luther.

"That would do it," said Alex. "You know, I've been thinking about your story and something doesn't make sense. Why not eliminate you with force?"

"They did blow up a building," said Luther.

"Yes but if something national or global is going on, wouldn't there be more people involved?"

Luther had never looked at it that way. When he had been sent after Alex, it was only their boss who was dirty. Only when Luther turned, did Kilmer bring in the agency.

"You think one of these men in the Core is a fuck up and he's covering his ass?"

"It's very likely," said Alex. "Which explains why you're not dead."

"Okay but which one? There are three: Henry Kilt, Greg Spector and Rylan Trot."

"Don't ask me. I just got here," said Alex.

"My plan is to eliminate them all," said Luther.

"Always a winner," said Alex, "but what if the one after you is the only one dirty? You'd be killing two innocent men."

"Who plotted against the U.S. and were part of a conspiracy to allow us to be attacked. I'd sleep okay."

"You don't have a lot of time," said Alex. "The Chicago rally is a month from now. So, what do you think of her?" he asked referring to his girlfriend.

"She's a knockout," said Luther, looking at the buxom dancer onstage. "How much does she know?"

"Just that I worked for the FBI," said Alex. "CIA would freak her out or she wouldn't believe it. And if I told her the truth, she'd run."

"I wouldn't blame her," said Luther. "People have a tendency to die around us."

"I suppose you'll be wanting my help," said Alex.

"Actually, I only need you to help me access Meyerson's money," said Luther. "I'll split it with you."

"I don't know if I should be relieved or pissed," said Alex. "Wait, I see. You're trying to get me to volunteer."

"Maybe. Or maybe I don't trust your skills anymore, which would make you want to volunteer to prove me wrong."

"Or," said Alex, "you really don't want me to come because you think I should be out of the game."

"Hard to tell with an agent," said Luther smiling.

"Fuck you," said Alex. "I'm going and you know why."

"I figured you were bored here."

"I have a guy who can clean that money," said Alex. "How much are we talking about?"

"Looks like seven or eight million," said Luther. "But he left a girl behind. I'd need most of it to go to them."

"You're getting soft," said Alex. "Okay, I'll get my guy on it but before we go, I need your help with something. I told you I keep busy here in Vegas. Well, it's a little more complicated than that. I kinda do an *Equalizer* thing."

"You mean *Burn Notice*," said Luther

"What's that?"

"Never mind, so you help people out?"

"Yes and I have a job before I can go to D.C. with you.

The performance ended and there was some applause from the sparse crowd.

"So, what name do you use here?" asked Luther.

"They just call me D."

Jayla Yonne, Alex's better half descended the stage and came over to them. As she did, Alex plunked down some bills and Jayla took them.

"So thoughtful," said Jayla. "You don't have to do that in here, you know."

"I'm a paying customer," said Alex. "This is a friend of mine. I could tell you his name but I'd have to kill you."

"I'm Jayla," she said and shook Luther's hand.

She was a mix of races and it was hard to place her. She wore a long blond wig and her eyes were green but they may have been contacts. Definitely part black, Luther thought and maybe Japanese.

Her body was tight and well-endowed up top, long legs but not much of an ass. Maybe not black, Luther corrected. Still, a very beautiful woman.

"You can call me David this trip," said Luther who still wore his disguise.

"David is going to help me with your friend's problem," said Alex. "And then I gotta go out of town for a bit."

Jayla just nodded but Luther could see the cold assessment in her gaze. She was trying to figure out just who he was and what was going on. Alex was a mystery and women loved that but they were always trying to solve it.

"You FBI, too? "she asked and she said 'FBI' with a measured amount of skepticism.

"No," said Luther.

Jayla laughed, showing perfect teeth. Luther smiled charmed by her flirtation. Alex looked as proud as any man is when he has a beautiful woman on his arm.

"Did D tell you what I do?" asked Jayla. "Or did he just say my woman is a hot piece of ass?"

"Jayla you know that's not fair," said Alex.

"He only said you dance here," said Luther. "But I'm curious about your actual job."

"Mathematician," said Jayla. "I work as a coder and algorithm specialist for Google."

"Doesn't sound as good as stripper," said Alex.

This got him an elbow in the ribs from Jayla who was proud of her talent.

"Well, my math teacher didn't look like you," said Luther.

"Easier to be pretty than smart," said Jayla "Who knows how many geniuses are on the pole."

"Just one," said Alex.

"I'm hardly a genius," said Jayla. "If I was, I could figure out how to help my friend."

"David and I are going to take care of that," said Alex.

Jayla smiled brightly. "Thank you."

"You're welcome," said Alex. "In fact, you should go now so we can talk."

"Okay, sweetie," said Jayla and she kissed him on the cheek. To Luther, she said: "Ask him what his nickname is out here."

She walked away and Luther did not try to hide his approval. She was gorgeous as she glided across the room.

"I'd be lying if I didn't say I was jealous," said Luther.

"She probably is a genius," said Alex. "She's eccentric, which is the only reason why her bosses let her do this."

"I've never seen you like this," said Luther. "Happiness doesn't suit you, really but I like it. So, what's the job?"

"Jayla's best friend hooked up with a fat cat who ran a brothel in the zone. When he died, he left her his license and grandfathered her in. Some guys called the Nathanson Brothers are trying to move in on her and they are playing rough. Last week, they set fire to one of her trailers while a girl was banging a guy. Needless to say, business has been down since then."

"There's no mob out here anymore," said Luther. "So, who are they?"

"Wannabes," said Alex. "Some locals trying to stake a claim and figured a widow was an easy mark. Prostitution is very lucrative and it's the gift that keeps on giving. You use it to fund everything else you're trying to do, maybe even buy into a smaller casino and set the stage for bigger ventures, all off a woman's back."

"So, what do they call you out here?" asked Luther.

"It's silly," and Luther swore he saw Alex blush.

"Come on, you know I'm not going to stop asking."

"The Ghost," said Alex. "I'm The Ghost."

****

Their first stop was with a man named Hector Vaccario. He was a financial analyst for several of the casinos. His real job was hiding and finding money. He'd worked for the big New York banks before the crash and had just gotten out by the seat of his pants.

Hector was a smallish man with a balding head that was a little misshapen. He wore expensive suits and talked very fast.

He had a little office on the strip close to The Wynn Complex. The place looked like crap from the outside but once in, it was like a palace.

"Mr. V will see you now," said Lisa, the receptionist whose boobs jutted out from her tight fitting suit.

They walked into Hector's office, which matched the outside decor. Alex and Luther sat at a very nice conference table.

"Mr. D, always good to see you," said Hector.

"I need a favor," said Alex. "I have funds in locked accounts that are being monitored. I need the funds released without tracers on the money."

Hector's brow furrowed. "Doable but costly," said Hector. "I can route it through Asia but you know what fuckin' crooks they are. You'd be lucky to have twenty bucks left. I can do it but you're gonna lose a lot of it." He paused and then added: "Unless…"

Alex sighed. "What is it now, Hector? Which ex-wife do you need handled?"

Hector had three exes and could not control himself around attractive women which made Vegas a real problem for him.

"Not an ex, her son, my stepson," said Hector. "He got into some trouble. He was hanging out with some guys and they accidentally shot at some cops. Hit one of them and he's in the hospital. Now the cops are all over him and Cara. They're going to run them out of town."

"He shot a cop?" asked Alex. "Jesus, Hector you know I don't like law enforcement."

"So your friend here, he doesn't talk?" asked Hector as he noticed Luther's steely looks.

"He's a client," said Alex.

"We take care of the kid's problem and you get our money for free," said Luther.

"Sure," said Hector.

Luther was sure he was lying about the difficulty of getting the funds.

"Where's the gun?" asked Luther. "I can assume he ditched it but somehow I don't think this kid is that smart."

"He brought it to me," said Hector. "I got that law degree on line three years ago and I passed the bar in Oregon and got reciprocity here, so it was all confidential."

Hector went to a wall safe, opened it and returned with a .9mm in a plastic baggie.

"I wiped it clean but I'm scared to ditch it," said Hector. "There are cameras all over this damned city."

Luther took the weapon and then gave Hector the accounts and institutions of Meyerson's funds.

"Man, this guy was really loaded," said Hector. "Okay, I can do this but it'll take a day or two."

"Make it a day," said Alex.

Alex and Luther exited Hector's office and headed to their car.

"Do I have to tell you my plan?" asked Luther.

"No," said Alex. "It's fairly simple."

"Cool," said Luther. "Two birds, one gun."

The next day, police swarmed a local bar called *The Baron's Lair* in Vegas owned by a man named Chenny Nathanson and his brother Robert.

They acted on an anonymous tip that the men who had wounded Nevada PD Officer Rick Hanson had bragged how they had shot the officer and blamed it on some stupid kids.

The police got a warrant and stormed the bar, doing a search that uncovered the weapon that shot officer Hanson in the establishment's safe.

Only Chenny Nathanson and his brother had access to the safe. Both swore they had never seen the gun.

It had been very easy for Luther and Alex to stage a break in and decode the safe in Nathanson's club. It was a cheap First Alert safe that had been sunk into a concrete floor.

Nathanson and his brother were both under indictment and even if they beat the charge, they'd never be able to run a brothel, a casino or hold a liquor license in Vegas.

Jayla had been overjoyed when she heard the news. She thanked Alex profusely and her friend had offered Alex and Luther free services at her brothel for a year. They had both respectfully declined.

Hector had freed up Luther's money as promised and Luther arranged for it to be split between Meyerson's lady friend and his family.

Hector was a creep but he was quite good at his job. He had come up with an ingenious way to get the money legally by using real estate escrow transfers.

A day later, Luther and Alex were on their way to D.C. They'd taken a southern route by car and would drive up from Florida.

It took extra time but they had anticipated how their enemies would be searching for them.

Luther had taken some of the money and restocked his weapons cache and bought other goodies from an arms dealer Alex knew.

Alex had established a very good group of contacts in the west. He had a good life but he would never leave Luther in the lurch on something like this. Alex did not wear his patriotism on his sleeve but he did believe in America and would die for it.

Washington's social season was beginning and so their targets would be in town. These men would never expect Luther to come after them given their power and high profiles. But they didn't know E-1 or the infamous Rule 225 which allowed any measure to restore order.

Bane was wrong. Luther was going to play this game and he was going to win.

≈≈≈≈≈≈≈≈≈≈≈≈≈≈≈≈≈≈≈≈≈≈≈≈≈≈≈≈≈≈≈

PART THREE:

THE AMERICAN GAME

"The ultimate operation is public yet secretive,
it cost very little but returns copious amounts
of wealth; it promises safety but is deadly to
your enemies; it runs on the will of those it sets
out to destroy and derives its greatest power
from the fact that it does not seem to exist."

- Black Ops Manual

≈≈≈≈≈≈≈≈≈≈≈≈≈≈≈≈≈≈≈≈≈≈≈≈≈≈≈≈≈

15

Waking Dead

A month ago,
Jagged light cut across the blackness, soundless, like
dangerous ideas, but it was pleasant, nothing like the
thoughts she'd had about death or anything she'd read; it was
inviting, soft, surrounded by music like a thousand distant
bells, a promise of something solid and quick to the touch, a
breath of...
What the fuck was she thinking?
She'd been killed, thought Sharon Bane. Gut shot and
poisoned to hasten her departure. She'd lost and now she was
going to the place where all killers went.
But she would not ask for forgiveness or mercy. She'd
known this day would come and she was ready to meet her
maker or whatever had caused us to come to this miserable
life.
The light came again and for a second, she saw shapes,
images. Human? And then she heard something behind the
thin music.
Voices?
The darkness fell on her again and this time, it was heavy
and final. It dropped like a weight onto her consciousness and
she let go of her struggle to go back.
She wanted to move on, see what was making that music,
go to that place and stand again with the power of her body.
The dark began to fade to gray, the light was coming back
only it did not cut a path, it was separating the dark...

****

Luther and Meyerson had left a badly bleeding
Sharon Bane with a steel ball near her heart and a body

filled with a drug called Pytalinol-C5, a synthetic compound that sped up the cardiovascular system.

Luther had given her an overdose that should have killed her. But what he didn't know was that Bane had been taking another compound, a performance enhancer, which fought the PC5 when her heart arrested, forcing it to keep working.

She'd taken the other substance so she could keep up with Luther. She had no idea that it would save her life.

Bane was technically dead but not so far gone that she could not be saved.

When her team arrived, they started her heart back up, while the PC5 kept trying to stop it. She arrested three more times on her way to the hospital where she was given a counter agent and stabilized.

She was weak and had suffered some brain damage. She'd had a little stroke, which had contorted the left side of her face, obliterating her muscle control. It looked like part of it was trying to slide off.

The doctors said there was nothing they could do to restore it. She would no longer be the beauty she was but at least she was not dead.

Bane lay in a hospital bed as doctors and government types fussed over her. Officially, she had been on a classified mission and was attacked by an unknown assailant.

To her contact from The Core, she had botched the assignment and allowed the target to escape.

The U.S. placed a local agent with her to make sure she didn't say anything while drugged that was classified.

What doctors didn't know was that agent was also authorized to kill Bane if she babbled anything vital.

All the while, Bane was returning to strength and buying time. When she was ready, she would hit the guard and scramble out of the facility. It would have to be at night. There were fewer people around then. She'd steal an ambulance, then ditch it when she was a good distance off. From there, she'd steal some clothes and then get some cash and hide until she could secure passage out of the country.

If she didn't get away, she would be debriefed and then killed as soon as they were certain she had given them all she knew about Luther and Meyerson's whereabouts.

Luther.

She had underestimated him. He was clever and resourceful but never did she think he would have put together her complicity. She still didn't know what had given her away. She had been so careful, she thought. She recounted every step she had taken. That fucker was good, she thought. He was the best.

She should have fucked him, she mused. He wanted her and she had always been curious about him. Luther was a hard man but they all liked pussy. But she had thrown out that possibility when they spoke of Cari. She could see on his eyes that they had fucked. Luther was clearly conflicted about Cari and that would make him more resistant to seduction.

On her third day in the hospital, her agent guard and all the doctors went away after lunch. This was not normal and she was left unattended.

This was it, she'd thought. She had not gotten strong enough to escape and so they were going to kill her. She waited, her vital signs going higher as the monitors beeped her stress.

The door to her room opened and a man entered. She had never seen him before and he did not look like and assassin or even an agency man.

The only way to describe would be neat. He was very clean and proper looking. His suit was immaculate, his hair perfect and his face was very common. He could have been anyone.

The Neat Man moved over to her bed and pulled up a chair.

"Why are you alive?" he asked casually. He sounded American.

"I tried to escape but I tripped a restraint counter and the projectile entered my chest. I was dying and in pain, so Luther overdosed me. I thought I was dead."

"You were," said the Neat Man. "In fact, you died three times according to what I've been told. What I need to know is if he did it on purpose."

"No, he tried to kill me," said Bane. "He was going to shoot me anyway. I know him."

"Yes, we know," said the Neat Man. "You and he were very close. Perhaps you two consummated on the mission and you compromised yourself."

"That didn't happen," said Bane defiantly.

"But you have entertained fucking him have you not?"

"Yes," said Bane not wanting to lie.

Mr. Neat was using a very old technique to see if she was compromised. He was going to ask her off-kilter things and watch her reaction. How she reacted would be the difference between life and death.

"You admire Green, correct?"

"Yes, I do."

"That is apparent because here you are," the Neat Man smiled at her. "Any other drug would have killed you but the one he used causes the heart to shut down which gave them just enough time to save you."

"No," said Bane getting his point. "Why would he do that?"

"To get you out of your situation. We think he tried to kill you, so we don't eliminate you for failing. It cost you but you are alive."

"Then I guess I'm fucked," said Bane, "because I can't prove he didn't."

"You were saved, Ms. Bane, because of a steroid in your system. I assume you took it voluntarily to help you perform."

"Yes," said Bane. "It's a cocktail of steroids and other things."

The Neat Man's countenance suddenly changed. His face hardened and eyes seemed to grow larger.

"Do you realize the threat Green poses to us?" he said.

"Yes," said Bane. "But he doesn't know the plan. He just has pieces of it."

"He was smart enough to figure out that you were compromised. By the way, how did he do it?"

"I don't know. I... I haven't been able to figure it out. I must have had a tell," she said with defeat in her tone.

"Green was our first choice for this, you know," said the Neat Man. "But he is a true believer. Such men are dangerous to life. Men like that are better killed than turned."

Bane said nothing. The Neat Man's assessment was over. He leaned back in his chair and just looked at her. He would leave and then the guard would come back and suffocate her or inject her IV with something. She wondered how they would do it. This time, when she entered the darkness, she would not come out.

"Send my body back home," said Bane. "I think I deserve a burial."

"We are sending you back out to get Green and Meyerson," said the Neat Man. "The doctors are going to help you get back to full health or as close as you can get. You still have value to us and we do not have time to turn another E-1 agent."

Bane was relieved. She sat up but felt a terrible rush of pain. She choked it down. She did not want him to think she was not up for it.

"If Luther is running with Meyerson, we can assume he will get out of the country," said Bane. "My first job was to find out if Meyerson had a copy of the information that we recovered from Cantini's home. So, if Luther is still with Meyerson, then it must exist."

"In America?" asked the Neat Man

"Yes," said Bane.
"Then that is where you are going."

16

The Core

Vienna, Virginia.

Luther and Alex settled just outside of the capitol. It was a dangerous proposition to be so close to the many operatives and surveillance systems, but it was a move that no one would anticipate.

Luther's mission was to find out the inciting event to this new operation and stop it. To do that, he had to take one of the leaders of the operational coup that rose to influence after 9-11 and interrogate him.

Once he stopped the event, he would be free and save his nation at the same time. And then he would kill all three of the men.

But should he? America had never been a true democracy for a long time. Certainly by the Spanish-American War, America was controlled by a small group of powerful men and companies.

These were the ones who pushed President McKinley into that conflict against his will. And so it had been since.

What made The Core evil as compared to those other men? They had used a terrorist attack to secretly steal power and guide a frightened nation and vengeful leaders. How was this any different from the way the nation had progressed in the past?

Alex had not batted an eye when Luther told him what he had discovered. Then again, this was the man who had seen the beginnings of a plan to subjugate Africa with a mutated virus.

"Who do we focus on first?" said Alex as they settled into the very spartan home they'd rented with some of Meyerson's funds.

"Kolt," said Luther. "Spector and Trott work out of New York. Kolt always stays down here."

"He feels more secure," said Alex. "I don't blame him. He's got a ton of secure measures and he's almost never alone but he does have one vice that makes him vulnerable. He loves these hookers down here and he likes to play. Man would do well in Vegas. So, how do we get to him?"

Luther set up his computer and accessed information on Henry Kolt.

Kolt was sixty-one and the son of Garrison Kolt III and the recipient of some very old money. He had a brother who was a TV producer and had been married three times. One of his wives had died under mysterious circumstances in a boating accident. She was the only one who did not have a prenuptial agreement.

These days, Kolt was single and kept company in public with several society women but his sexual activities were divided between two high class call girl agencies, one called Tinsel and the other Patina.

Tinsel was a legit escort service and did a regular business with models and actress types. The prostitution was handled individually and the money kicked back without tracers.

Patina was actually a private, five-star restaurant in the area. The hookers were ordered along with dinner reservations and coupling done off campus. It was said that on any given night, you could find many political luminaries there.

"How does a clown like this get to be such a powerful man?" asked Alex.

"I never look at current brokers for their influence," said Luther. "His father was a third. Let's check out the grandfather. He would have been in the dough before the great war."

Garrison Kolt II was a soldier and mercenary. The son of a cattle farmer and miner, he had gone to war in

WWI. It was rumored that he had killed his commanding officer when he refused to fire on the enemy. Kolt received a Silver Star and other medals and rose to the rank of General at forty-two.

But Garrison Kolt's real talent was trading on the black market during wars. He trafficked with the U.S. and their enemies, supplying both sides in conflicts. He became an oil baron and one of the first men to invest in technology, founding a company called Icon Systems.

He later served in the government and established monetary policy as well as guidelines for commodities trading. But he never wanted to head a department. Kolt was always a behind the scenes player, a kingmaker, never a king.

By the time he died and left the business holdings to his sons, he was estimated to be worth millions.

Henry Kolt pushed his brother, Timothy, out of the business but provided generously for him. Kolt took over and like his grandfather, kept away from the spotlight and obvious power.

Greg Spector was the lead partner of Spector, Danker & Travers. It was a law firm and lobbyist group located out of New York, Chicago and D.C. But that was a mere sideline for Spector who was a self-made billionaire in real estate and medical technology.

Spector was a colonel in the first Gulf War and was widely suspected in the disappearance of a flat bed with a billion dollars on it. The rumor was he killed the people it was supposed to buy off and the government was none the wiser.

Spector allegedly washed the money in Switzerland and Germany and then bought up land close to places where he knew America would bomb. Those lands grew in value and he traded on the equity to buy into Generast Labs, a medtech firm and Holliwell, a noted arms supplier.

Spector had only been married once and adopted his new wife's two kids. Unlike Kolt, he was quite conservative and was known to be somewhat of a recluse.

Rylon Trott was the youngest of the *troika* at forty-five. His grandfather, Oliver, was a former army colonel turned bootlegger along with Joe Kennedy Sr. back in the 1900's.

Oliver sold cocaine, opium and other drugs until they became illegal after the Food and Drug Act.

He then quickly started *Pankerhaus*, a pharmaceutical company and dealt in the new controlled substances.

Oliver left the company to his son, Danko, Rylon's father and *Pankerhaus's* name was changed to Revilo, his grandfather's name spelled backwards.

With massive profits from the now legal drugs, the Trott family invested in everything and by time young Rylon was born, they were wealthy beyond measure.

Danko Trott was a legendarily cruel man who had raised his only son to rule with an iron fist. He physically disciplined his son and put him into a military boarding school and groomed him to be a leader and businessman.

Danko was known to be heartless and famously attended a meeting the day his wife died. He was also a health nut who had lived to be 94 years old.

Rylon married a former actress whose family had vast holdings. Danko had approved of the combined fortunes.

Rylon was always interested in politics but like the others, never wanted to hold office. Vantage, his family's lobbying firm controlled Super PACs that were involved in every national election since LBJ.

Luther noted that in every case, there was a strong military influence in the family which had led to their fortunes. He recalled Eisenhower's famous speech about the military industrial complex. These three guys were definitely in that circle.

Spector and Trott were family and businessmen. Kolt was the one, the playboy, the weak link.

"Kolt's a regular at Patina," said Luther. "That's where we take him, tonight."

"We got specs on the place?" asked Alex.

Luther showed him a diagram. Patina was like a fortress. It was a converted private club set up on a hill. The nearest home to it was a quarter mile away. There was one road in and one road out.

"The back of the place faces a wall and that's where they'll fall back on security," said Alex.

"We come in there then," said Luther. "They'll be men posted."

"I know what you're thinking," said Alex. "But we have to employ lethal measures. Any security will have training, may even be former agency. We don't want to take any chances."

"Agreed," said Luther.

They formulated their plan. It would have to be fast but it could work if they executed well.

Luther's secure phone sounded. He checked.

"Agency," he said to Alex.

"Once you answer, will they know where you are?"

"No, I have it routed." Luther answered the call. "Ten, still blind."

"Don't give me that shit," said the woman on the other line.

Luther and Alex were briefly shocked at the sound of the voice. They knew that voice.

"Adelaide?" said Luther.

"I want you to come in," said Adelaide Gibson.

She was the last head of E-1, a retired agent who had helped Luther take down their corrupt boss. After the fall of E-1, she'd gone to work for the agency in the prestigious job of Regional Director.

"I can't," said Luther. "Circumstances."

"Bane's missing," said Adelaide. "Where is she?"

Luther knew better than to give any information while blind on a mission. Adelaide was trying to extract anything out of him. He had to play her as best he could, pretend that he didn't know anything.

"If that's true, I'm sorry," said Luther. "I can't say anything further."

"She doesn't answer her calls," said Adelaide. "That means, she's with you and doesn't want to communicate, which makes no sense, or she can't because she's dead."

There was silence on the line. Adelaide was a friend and she knew Luther would not divulge anything to her but she had a job to do and she might be monitored on this call.

"Someone blew up a fleabag motel in your hometown. Not the kind of thing drug dealers do," said Adelaide. "Don't suppose you know anything about that, either."

Luther was silent.

"I can't help you if you don't trust me," said Adelaide.

"Ten blind," said Luther.

"Fine," said Adelaide. "The agency isn't responsible for your actions and if you do anything, we'll disavow you, just like in the goddamned movies. Be careful, son, there may be no tomorrows."

She hung up.

"Feisty as ever," said Alex.

"She gave code," said Luther. "She wants me to know that people are watching me on the other side. That's why she mentioned Detroit. The agency doesn't watch for you when you go blind. And she never calls me son. That means tomorrow they will start looking for me. *No tomorrows.*"

"Man, she's good," said Alex. "I remember her being the old lady with the big gun in reception."

"But if she's calling," said Luther. "It means we have to move."

17

Distractions

Pimmit Hills, Virginia.

Luther and Alex had been watching the hilltop restaurant, Patina, since dawn. It was quite picturesque, nestled on its perch overlooking a small valley outside the capitol.

They went over their plan again and again until they each were tired of hearing it. Repetition, agents knew was the brain's way of engaging all of the subconscious mechanisms that triggered instinct.

He had done this with Bane in Evora, Luther thought. And though it was standard, he couldn't help thinking this was a bad omen.

Still, it was good to be working with Alex again, Luther thought. They laughed and told war stories, which to an outsider would have sounded grisly and demented.

Luther felt a little guilty for baiting Alex on the mission. Not many agents got out of the game in one piece and many of the ones who did usually became bitter, violent old men who could not turn off the kill switch which eventually destroyed their lives.

He didn't want that for Alex Deavers and he didn't want it for himself. Luther vowed that when this was over, he would make a change and begin planning his retirement. All the more reason to be successful, he thought. If he failed in this mission, the U.S. might not be the place to live anymore.

Night fell and the guests began to arrive. It was amazing that there was a high class whore house right in the middle of American power. On the other hand, it made sense. Politicians and hookers were really in the same business when you thought about it.

Luther and Alex waited an hour for the cocktail party to begin and then moved quickly toward the restaurant from the rear, dressed in dark suits like the other security men.

The first thing they needed would be mobile scan deflectors to mix with the security personnel.

Patina issued a metal computerized badge, which housed a chip that sent a pulse to the central security unit at the facility. The code was changed daily and all security men had updated chips on their lapels. As you moved about, you were constantly checked. They had to lift two of these in order to execute their plan.

But before they could get the deflectors, they needed to disable the rear perimeter scanners. They were crude motion detectors, which would alert security of anything approaching that was larger than a squirrel.

Thankfully, Patina didn't have cameras for obvious reasons and cell phone pics were banned.

Luther pulled a jammer and began to search for the scanner frequency. Once he found it, he jammed the scanner, which would make those watching think all was well. He set the jammer and then he and Alex moved forward toward their targets.

There were three guards at the rear and they had to be dispatched quickly. Patina did checks every quarter hour and so they would have fifteen minutes before their elimination of these guards turned into the distraction they needed to grab Kolt.

Luther signaled to Alex to take out the left guard. He would take the other two. They waited until a security check to give themselves optimal time.

"*Checkpoint epsilon,*" said Central Security.

"*Green epsilon,*" said one of the rear security men.

Alex jumped the left guard and disabled him with a groin kick and a knife to the throat and inner thigh.

Luther took one guard in a similar fashion and the other with a silenced shot.

They removed the deflector badges and headsets, put them on, then moved quickly to the rear of the restaurant and entered through a service door that led to a basement.

The odor of onions and garlic was strong. They moved inside and surfaced in the rear of the noisy kitchen.

"Checkpoint alpha," said Central Security.

"Green alpha," said forward security.

This was the first checkpoint. They had roughly ten minutes now.

Luther entered first, casually walking in. No one noticed him. Alex followed and they both moved quickly into a back room.

This was the fat cats' lair. Luther noticed several congressmen and a CNN correspondent.

And there nestled in the middle, telling a story to rapt onlookers was Greg Spector, one of the three alleged leaders of The Core.

Spector was very tall at about six foot six and had a full head of thick, gray hair. He held a long cigar and a brandy as he told his story.

Luther and Alex both saw him but did not react. Luther had a clean shot at the bastard but that was not their mission, not yet.

The inside security scanner swept past them and hit their badges. They were good.

Luther and Alex began to look for Kolt. It was the pre-dinner hour and the mostly male crowd was assembled in the front. They moved that way.

Luther and Alex entered the main room, where a cocktail party was going on. A larger group of powerbrokers was in this room and the chatter rose accordingly.

Suddenly, a group of young, beautiful men and women entered. There was a small buzz and the energy level in the room went up.

"Left forward, beta," said Central Security.

"Green beta," said a guard.

This was the second checkpoint. Eight minutes left.

The hookers began to circulate, when Luther spotted Kolt. He was holed up in a corner and had a personal guard, a very large man with a buzz cut and a goatee, next to him.

Kolt was a handsome man who probably knew it. He was lean and immaculately dressed. His hair was salt and pepper and swept back in the euro style. He looked a little like the basketball coach, Pat Riley.

Luther was in position and ready. Working in a crowded environment was not his favorite thing. Innocent people might be hurt and that was never good.

When the rear guards did not report, there would be an alert and the room would clear. In the confusion, Alex would take out Kolt's guard and Luther would grab Kolt.

Alex caught Luther's attention and nodded to a far corner. There, Luther saw Rylon Trott all alone, sitting on the arm of a chair, checking his phone. His youngish face and long hair made him look like a kid compared to most of the men in the place.

An alarm went off in Luther's head. All three men were here. Coincidence, or was something big going on in D.C.?

Luther recalled that Congress was in session and various State Dinners were being held, still he didn't know for sure. He suddenly missed Meyerson's perfect memory powers. He would have known or guessed why all three players were in the same place.

Luther turned back to Alex, nodded and then Alex walked into position near Kolt's guard.

Luther circled the other way round, moving past a woman who sidled up next to Trott and began chatting him up.

"Right forward, gamma," said Central Security.

"Green gamma," said a guard. Five minutes left.

Suddenly, there was an explosion outside the house. The place was rocked and the floor shook.

Luther and Alex both instinctively knew it was not an attack, but a distraction, one that was not of their making. Someone else was here on deadly business, he thought.

Luther watched as the people in the room panicked. The alarm went off and everyone headed for the exits.

Then he saw a ghost pull a gun and point it at Rylon Trott's head.

****

Fifteen minutes before Luther spotted her, Sharon Bane was marveling at being invisible. She got out of a car and walked toward Patina.

She'd lost her hair and now sported a short cut. She was dressed in a tight, one-piece dress. Her face was no longer pretty because of the trauma. It had lost is full, healthy look. Her skin had become a little blotchy and her face generally sagged on one side. Makeup fixed the surface but the muscle damage was something else.

She had gotten that fixed as best she could. She wore what looked to be a hearing aid but was really a nerve stimulator that sent small electrical pulses to the side of her face and kept the muscles taut.

Without it, she'd look like the Phantom of the Opera. With it, she was just an ordinary woman.

The forward guard checked her badge and it was good. The special badge allowed her to carry a weapon, which she had on the inside of her long trench.

"*Green alpha,*" she heard the other guard say.

She got no preference from men around her. No more admiring looks or flirtatious lines. They looked at her, then right through her.

Her body was still great and a few of the men ogled her as she stepped in her high heels and short dress, but no one *saw* her.

Bane slipped inside and began to scan the crowd. She could not help but to feel upset. She missed the attention and even though it was childish, she could not shake the feeling.

The women didn't give her catty glances or their preference, either. That was one of the secrets pretty girls knew, that women loved beautiful women, too. It wasn't a lesbian thing. It was like how a man admires a professional athlete.

She was just another face now and for tonight, that suited her just fine.

She pulled a detonator from her sleeve.

Bane did not see her target in the outer area. He would be in the main cocktail room and so she moved that way.

She felt another electrical pulse go into her face as she stopped to let the cadre of male and female hookers walk by.

Good, she thought. She would follow them in and as all these old goats drooled over the fresh meat, she'd spot her target and execute her mission.

The Neat Man had told her to eliminate Rylon Trott. She did not ask why but did inquire what it had to do with Luther Green and the operation.

She had been told not to question him, that the elimination of Trott would set the stage for the end of her mission.

Bane moved into the larger room. She spotted her target as one of the hookers went over to him.

She hit the detonator. The explosion was deafening and as she pulled her weapon on Trott. She saw the shock and fear in his face, knowing he was about to die.

****

Luther saw Sharon Bane but she did not see him. He was shocked but did not have time to linger on it.

Luther shoved a running man into her and her shot missed Trott and hit the hooker next to him.

Trott yelled as Bane hit the floor and was trampled by running people.

Trott's guard grabbed him and headed for the door. He swept people aside with his big arm as he moved his boss toward freedom.

Luther saw Alex move over and suddenly the big guard buckled and fell as Alex had probably tasered him.

"I got you, sir!" Alex said as he grabbed Trott's arm. Trott did not question it. He had just escaped death and he was trying to get out.

Luther saw Kolt being rushed out of the room by his guards. It was too late.

"Mr. Trott, this way!" said Luther as he grabbed Trott's other arm and rushed out of the room.

They were both thinking the same thing, Trott was marked and that made him their man.

****

Bane scrambled to her feet, holding her gun amid the chaos. Her coat was torn and her dress was hiked up. She scanned the room but did not see her target.

"Goddammit!" She hissed and she struggled to stand in her high heels.

Bane ran to the door but was stopped by a barrage of people. She removed the silencer from her gun and fired it into the ceiling, parting the crowd.

"Move!" She yelled as she squeezed herself through the door, gun out in front of her.

****

Outside the restaurant, Luther and Alex rushed Trott to a line of cars.

"This way, sir!" said Alex.

"My car," said Trott.

"No time for that," said Luther. "We have to get you out of here. That shooter may be close by."

"I have to call my family," said Trott. "They'll be worried if they hear about this."

"When we get safely away," said Luther. "Right now, we have to get you away from here."

Luther shoved a man from a BMW, pushed Trott inside and got in the back next to him. While he did this, he lifted Trott's cell phone.

Alex jumped into the driver's seat and took off, going with a flood of cars leaving the place.

****

Bane rushed to the door and looked around at the chaos but did not see her prey. She cursed silently, breathing heavily.

Bane went down the line of cars, past the hysterical men and women, looking for her prey. She did not find him. After ten minutes, police and fire were there and she knew she had to leave quickly.

"Fuck," she said. "Fuck me."

"My thoughts exactly," said a man from behind her.

Bane turned to see Greg Spector, The Neat Man, standing calmly, flanked by his security team. His cigar was still smoking.

Gary Hardwick179.

18

The Americas

The BMW sped along the narrow road away from
the chaos at Patina. Alex drove quickly as police
vehicles passed by the other way.

In the back, Luther sat next to Trott who was coming
down from his panic.

Bane was alive, which meant she was the one who
killed Meyerson and blew up The Palm. She'd placed
the tracker in Meyerson and so it all made sense.

He was angry but could not deny that he was a little
pleased that she had survived.

What didn't make sense was Bane on a mission to
kill Rylon Trott. No doubt she was going to execute
him amid the chaos at the restaurant. Why was the
question.

"That woman... she tried to kill me," said Trott his
voice still shaking a little.

"If you have a danger contingency with your family,
I suggest you initiate," said Luther.

Trott reached for his cell phone but found that it was
gone. Luther handed Trott his own cell phone.

"Use my phone, sir."

Trott took the phone and dialed.

"Honey," said Trott. "We're on vacation. Grab Debra
and go."

"What?!" said the woman on the other end, her voice
rising.

"You're not supposed to say *what*," said Trott. "Just
do like we practiced. I'll see you at the safe point."

Trott hung up and took a deep breath. "Okay, swing
around to Dulles."

"No sir," said Luther taking his cell away. "We're
not your security or Patina's."

"What?" said Trott as he seemed to realize for the first time that he did not know either man. Fear crept into his visage. "Who are you guys with? Where are my men?"

"We are going to switch vehicles," said Luther, "because this one has a tracker in all likelihood."

"Who are you with?" asked Trott. "Are you agency? What is this?"

"This is do what he says," said Alex from the front of the car.

Alex drove onto a side road off the main street leading to the restaurant. He then went off road, back to their vehicle. He pulled the BMW over.

He and Luther got out, taking Trott. Luther scanned Trott, then his cell phone.

"He's clean," said Luther.

"Whatever you want, I can pay it," said Trott.

"We know that," said Alex. "But we don't want money."

"We have more work to do," said Luther "And I can't take the chance that you'll run."

"I'm not going to run," said Trott.

"Sorry," said Luther. "Nothing personal."

And then he jabbed Trott with a hypo. Trott fell limp.
Luther placed Trott in their SUV, turned off his cell and then drove away.

Alex took the BMW and they drove closer to the city and left the BMW in a dicey neighborhood. That would lead someone on a merry chase if the car was stolen.

They drove back to the safehouse together and Luther's mind was already calculating the change in the mission.

"Just my professional opinion," said Alex, "but you could have done a better job killing Sharon Bane."

"I couldn't believe it," said Luther. "But she didn't see us, I don't think, so she can't advise whoever she's working for."

"When I saw her draw down on Trott," said Alex. "I knew we were after the wrong guy."

"We have to get all the info we can and we have to get it fast," said Luther.

"Nice move warning his wife and kid," said Alex. "I wouldn't have."

"If I'm right," said Luther, "whoever tried to hit him will go after his loved ones. If they do and his wife is gone, he will trust us."

"That's a big maybe after knocking the guy out."

"I said I was sorry," said Luther.

They reached the safehouse which had a garage connected to it. Luther did not think Trott was personally dangerous and so there was no need to tie him up. But they did sweep him again but found no trackers.

They got him inside and made him as comfortable as they could. Alex turned on the TV and waited to see the coverage. The media was saying that there was a fire at a local restaurant, that's all. Nothing about an explosion or a gunshot. Made sense. Any of those things would draw too much attention.

After ten minutes, Trott came to.

"Jesus… what was that stuff?" said Trott.

"A little drug that put you in a nice REM sleep for about a half hour," said Luther. "Developed by your father's company, actually."

"Oh, the irony," said Alex.

"Again," said Trott. "what's this about? Who are you?"

"First," said Luther. "Let's talk about what you do know. You know an attempt was made on your life at Patina. You know that we stopped it and saved your life. We got you out safe and warned your family. Now, I want you to call and check in with your wife on speaker, please."

Luther tossed Trott his cell phone. Trott dialed hastily.

"Honey," said Trott. "Are you and Debra safe?"

"Yes,"said Trott's wife. She sounded afraid. "Are you okay?"

"I'm fine," said Trott, looking at Luther.

"The house," said Trott's wife. "After we left, men with guns came and... they shot some of the staff. The police are there. Who were they, Rylon?"

Trott's face went slack as he realized the implications of this. Someone wanted to wipe him out and Luther could tell that Trott knew who it was.

"It's most likely a kidnaping attempt," said Trott. "Thank God we're all safe."

"When are you coming home?" asked his wife.

"Soon," said Trott, taking another glance at the two agents. "I'll call back in an hour. Be safe."

"Okay. I love you."

"I love you, too," said Trott. He hung up.

"Touching," said Alex.

"He always such an asshole?" said Trott referring to Alex.

"Yes," said Luther.

"Okay," said Trott. "You have my attention, fellas. Do I get names or is this super secret agent man shit?"

"I have some bad news," said Luther. "Do you have a mistress?"

"Yes," said Trott with just a little hesitation. "Two of them. Why?"

"They're most likely dead," said Luther. "If your enemies are playing by standard rules, they have been planning this for months and have taken every contingency. So, those women have been taken and if you do not show, they will be killed."

"Assuming they are women," said Alex, which got him a nasty look from Trott.

"An E-1 agent was sent to kill you tonight," said Luther.

"E-1," said Trott. "There is no E-1 anymore. Everyone knows that."

"One of my former colleagues tried to kill me earlier this year," said Luther. "She failed and I thought I'd killed her. Apparently, I didn't, because she was the one who tried to shoot you tonight."

"So the real question is," said Alex. "Who the fuck did you piss off."

"Jesus," said Trott quietly. "Fucking E-1."

"I love the respect in the way you said that," said Alex.

"Okay," said Trott, "How do I know this isn't some elaborate hoax. You could be CIA or those fucking Red Dogg assholes hired by an enemy. Maybe the woman with the gun is your partner."

"The Core," said Luther. "That's why we're here and it doesn't matter who we work for. It's what you've done that matters now."

Trott's eyes widened and he tried to remain calm.

"Haven't heard that name for a while," said Trott.

"We came to Patina to grab Henry Kolt," said Luther. "We thought he was the man we needed to end our mission but now, I think it's you."

"Was it Kolt who wanted you hit?" asked Alex.

Trott's eyes wandered for a moment. He was thinking, putting pieces of some intimate puzzle together.

"Not Kolt," said Trott. "Spector."

Luther and Alex shared a look. Now they knew who Bane was working for. Gregory Spector.

"You need to know what we know," said Luther.

Luther told Trott everything they knew thus far, about the abduction of Meyerson, the damning information on 9-11, the chase through Michigan and their acquiring of some knowledge of a plan to execute a violent event on American soil to effect some kind of social or political change in the U.S.

"I knew this day might come," said Trott resignedly. "I'm the man in your story who commissioned Carl Jennings from the DOD to get evidence on General Davenport, Bob Lefts and Alicia Ford. I knew Jennings was friends with Meyerson and I hoped Meyerson would just memorize the information and we'd always have some threat we could use internally. I didn't know he'd make a goddamned recording and steal the prelims on the plan."

"First," said Luther. "Why?"

"I was a kid back after 9-11," said Trott. "My father, asshole that he was, planned to do something that was repugnant to me. I mean, he did a lot of shit but this was too much. I thought it was my duty…"

Trott's voice trailed off. Luther and Alex said nothing. They just waited for him. He was working things through.

"People have no idea what goes on in the real world," Trott continued. "The United States changed everything in world politics. Freedom is a great thing. Still, men have always sought to control what people do, men like my father and so, we've always had these councils, cabals, these star chambers of undue influence. I guess I found my inner patriot because I couldn't stomach their plan."

"Nice speech," said Alex. "But we need to know about what The Core is planning."

"There is no Core," said Trott with a small bitter laugh. "Not anymore, at least. The organization you refer to now has no official name." He took a long pause, then a breath and then: "The events of September 11 were used as the beginning of a bigger plan."

Luther and Alex had been watching him for signs of deception. So far, they saw none. Trott was afraid and exhausted but either he was telling the truth or he was the best liar Luther had ever seen.

"What's the operation?" asked Luther. "We only got pieces of it in our intel."

"To end the U.S. as we know it," said Trott. "Split the nation like before the Civil War, only this time not north and south but along ideological, economic and religious lines."

There was silence for a moment as this idea settled into Luther's mind. The U.S. was just that, a group of individual and sovereign states united under a federal banner. Theoretically, any one state or group of states could remove itself from the rest. The South tried and the results were disastrous, still they did secede initially.

"What's the inciting event?" asked Luther, breaking the quiet.

"Holy Rebels in Chicago," said Trott. "Terrorism would not be enough this time. We needed something that transcended violence and fear, something that people would think was almost supernatural. We needed a sign from God."

"Pretty tall order," said Alex.

"I thought so, too," said Trott calmly. "And then the motherfuckers did it. They fuckin' did it!" Trott laughed darkly, then continued: "We were told that a weapons system was developed that would seem to make all of those thousands of people at the rally disappear."

Luther and Alex shared a look. Trott still seemed to be telling the truth. In fact, the look on his face suggested that he was afraid.

"So people would think it was biblical," said Luther. "Every religion has a scenario for the end of time. Did they do a test? It would have been hard but they had to know it would work in real life conditions."

"Of course they did," said Trott. "You may remember that after we bombed Iraq, there were over a million refugees scattered across the Middle East and Europe. The bands were roughly in groups of ten to twenty thousand. A very small group, fifteen hundred traveling across Saudi Arabia went missing and it was widely rumored that they died in a freak sandstorm, bodies buried. But I saw footage taken with a night vision camera. They were there in an encampment and then, there was a flash of light and they were gone, all of them."

Trott paused in his story, his expression was one of pure fear now.

"I almost shit my pants," Trott continued. "I told myself it was a hoax, a special effect. But then they did another one in broad daylight. Africa. A guerrilla platoon in the North about a hundred of them, flash and gone. I remember Spector, that fuck was laughing, saying 'Excellent, excellent,'" He imitated the Neat Man's voice.

"How does it work?" asked Alex.

This was a test question. If Trott had an explanation, then it would be more likely that he was making this up. In a planned, long-term covert operation, specific information of the method of destruction was limited. In fact, it was calculated to keep powerful men in the dark, so that they could not give out damaging information and retain plausible deniability. If Trott did not know the specifics of the weapon, well, they might all be fucked.

"They don't tell you that," said Trott matter of factly. "You know how it goes. Nobody knows anything."

Luther knew that a weapon like this could be developed in secret given our current state of technology. It probably had limits and needed certain conditions. Just like the refugees, the people at the rally would be stationary, huddled close together in one place with defined boundaries

"Motherfuck us all," said Alex.

"Death toll estimate post event?" asked Luther. This would be information in a standard operational report.

"Another one to three million," said Trott. "Riots, panic, protests. Urban assault to contain violence, focused on the blacks and Latinos. Martial law, gun confiscation, the whole nine. We believed the people will rise up but over time, they will choose to live among like minded people in the three new sub nations, which would just form naturally with a little help from the government and certain corporations."

"So will these three Americas be separate countries?" asked Alex.

"No," said Trott. "More like a working division with sections controlled by ideologies or commerce. If the divisions didn't work together, we'd lose power. But there would still be a central government, just not as big."

"But with weakened states, the government would be even more powerful than before," said Luther.

"One Ring to rule them all," said Trott with more nervous laughter. "Just like in the book."

He was referring to *Lord Of The Rings*, where the evil Sauron possessed the One Ring which controlled the others and turned them into his unwilling slaves.

"Religion and farming will dominate the South," Trott continued. "Banking, military concerns and the central government will dominate the East and the West will be the center of technology and agnosticism. They will all work together but be treated like sovereign nations in the end."

"Why murder people to do that?" asked Alex absently. "Oh, what am I thinking?" He corrected himself.

"It's the only thing we understand," said Luther. "Murder always motivates."

"This event will divide the nation for a greater good," said Trott. "Or that's what we thought. It's supposed to reinvigorate religious values and serve as the catalyst for people letting go of the old Constitution and building a new one. It sounded good at first but these new Americas will just be places where more people will be oppressed and freedom will die. I saw that when my father told me about it and asked me to take over for him before he died. I couldn't do it."

"We want to see it, the plan," said Luther. "I know you have access to a copy."

Luther brought his computer to Trott.

"If I access my files, they will know where I am," said Trott. "This place will be surrounded in minutes or maybe they just lob a bomb in here."

"I know," said Luther. "I have a method for access."

Luther took the computer and went into his backdoor on the agency's system. He bypassed Trott's security, which was not surprisingly using the same safeguards as the government.

Trott coded in his elaborate passwords. Ten minutes into the hack, Luther called up the plan:

TACTICAL AND OPERATIONAL PLAN
FOR THE DIVISION OF THE UNITED STATES.

Preamble

The interests of the people have been increasingly divergent for over a century now. The nation has been so divided, resources stretched so thin, that drastic action needs to be taken. The races and ideologies have grown so hostile, that to preserve the union, we must divide it. This can be done through a tactical operation which uses social conflict, religion and mythology to push the citizenry into distinct camps, of religious social order and technological progressivism. This will necessitate another milestone event on American soil, one that not only suggests earthly conflict but spiritual intervention. Without this event, we project

*that the nation will falter within the century
and be absorbed by foreign nations through
international corporate action and domestic
land acquisition. The United States as we
know will end. We can save the union, if we
end it on our own terms.*

There was a makeshift map of the new America, showing the new Americas, a thick line running along Minnesota curving around Missouri and Arkansas then over Mississippi and down the Alabama/Georgia border to the sea. The other line started between Montana and Idaho in the North then swung around Wyoming, Colorado and the New Mexico/Texas border into the Gulf. Hawaii and Alaska would belong to the West all other territories to the East.

"This will really fuck up the NFL," said Alex.

"I told them it wouldn't work," said Trott, "that despite our differences, the people would band together against division. They said it didn't matter, that even if people resisted, that all they'd do is complain about it even as they went along with it."

"They believe our will has been broken," said Luther. "They're wrong about that."

"How long is the operation?" asked Alex.

"Looks like it spans almost a half century," said Luther, "but the basic plan will be accomplished in the next twenty years after the event."

"They can't do Chicago now," said Trott. "They know I'm alive."

"They will have a contingency plan," said Alex. "But we're not going to give them a chance to vaporize anyone. You can go," said Luther.

"What?" said Trott. "What about me? They'll surely try to kill me now."

"Call the men most loyal to you," said Luther, "and arrange to go into hiding. It's your only chance if we fail. We're going to need one more thing from you tonight. Instructions will be sent to your cell in a few minutes."

"Go meet your family," said Alex. "Keep your head down."

Trott walked out, raising the phone to his ear. After he was out of earshot, Alex went to a shelf and checked the camera he'd placed there.

"Still recording," said Alex. "We got him on record." Alex turned off the mini camera.

"Good," said Luther. "Let's get moving."

Luther and Alex began to pack up. The night was still young and they needed to get to Spector and Bane before either of them caught on to who had saved Rylon Trott.

If it all worked out, Bane and Spector would be dead before the sun rose.

19

Clients

Gregory Spector waited patiently for his teleconference to begin. These people were damned fearful and secretive about everything but he had to inform them of the current status and request permission to move, or he might be on the business end of a gun next time.

By rule, they could not begin a conference until their encryption was secured and double checked and each participant was on the line.

Spector watched the huge monitor in his office in this Virginia home. It looked like the President's War Room with its computer terminals and long conference table. The monitor almost covered one wall. All six slots were dark. Of course, Trott's window would not be open, he thought, not tonight. So, there would only be five clients.

He did not know how Rylon Trott had escaped him. He had planned to assassinate him at the club, so that no one would dare give any information. What man wanted the world to know he was at a known high end hooker restaurant?

Trott was a punk, a bleeding heart rich kid who did not earn his money. If he had, he would have had much blood on his hands, then he would have understood what was at stake.

But Spector did not think the kid would betray them the way he did. Trott had stolen information from Spector's computer system and gave it to Meyerson through an intermediary. Meyerson was found out but it took all these years to find out the source was Trott, the snot-nosed liberal.

"Client one, ready," said his computer system in its female British accent. One person was ready.

Spector wished Patina had video feeds. That would have told him who saved Trott. Unfortunately, it was policy not to do any recording or take any pictures.

His back up plan had also failed. When his hit team came to Trott's home, his wife and daughter were gone. Obviously he had a mole in his organization.

They did manage to grab his girlfriends but Trott didn't care about them, so they would be released unharmed. Both women had placed calls to Trott but his phone had been turned off and the car he escaped in had been found in the heart of D.C.'s black neighborhoods, an obvious decoy while he got out of town.

"Clients two and three, ready."

It was possible he'd been kidnapped but that would not explain his wife ghosting. Trott was a smart man.

Spector slammed his fist down on a console hard. Everything had gone so well up until now. Bane had failed him and he would kill her after the event was rescheduled. Right now, her only job was to find Trott.

"Client two has withdrawn. Rechecking encryption."

Bane had been one of his favorites for over the last year as she was slowly seduced by money and power. She was sexy, adventurous and willing to do anything to get her way. It was easy to turn her to his employ with a load of cash and a promise of power in the new order.

He'd thought about killing Luther Green's family but they were under a protective order that if violated would bring a lot of heat even for him. He didn't need that. The government would be more cooperative in a year or two, he thought.

"Client two now, ready."

Green had been his first choice but a check of his background showed he was not the one. Spector didn't

understand why a black man had such loyalty to the
government. They usually did not because of history
but Green was an anomaly, a black patriot with red
white and blue blood in his veins.

Because Trott had escaped, Spector had to up his
timetable for the event. They would not be able to wait
for Chicago. They had to go to one of their backups and
it looked like the Eastern Christian Conference in
Pennsylvania was the one. There would only be
twenty-five thousand there but that would be good
enough. There would also be Mennonites and Quakers
at the EEC, that was a nice touch.

"Client four, ready."

The division of the nation was a brilliant idea. Given
the current deterioration of values and the new tech
economy, this was the only way to insure America's
continued dominance in the world.

No one knew that the origins of the action were in
Nazi Germany and Japan. Had the Axis won the war,
America would have been divided into thirds with the
Germans ruling the East and the Japanese the west. In
the middle of the nation, would be a neutral zone,
belonging to both conquering nations.

"Client five, ready."

"About goddamned time," said Spector. "Client six
will not be joining us. There was an incident tonight. I
am client seven, ready."

"Checking... All clients approve. Video."

The massive monitor came on and Spector faced five
men whose faces were obscured. Even though they all
knew each other, this was a precaution against hacks of
any kind.

Spector always got a tiny chill when he saw the
faceless men.

"Gentlemen," said Spector. "An unfortunate incident
tonight necessitates a timetable change."

"Goddamned right it does," said Client Three who
Spector recognized as Henry Kolt.

"Client Six is gone and I have reason to believe he has betrayed us. The matter is being attended to, but I am here to ask permission to go forward with Operation Free Will at another location."

"Is Client Six dead?" Asked Client One.

"Negative," said Spector, "but he will be soon enough. Details of this are best left unknown at this time. I need agreement to move to the new plan, which will occur sooner than we all wanted. It will have a lower initial kill ratio but the aftermath death toll numbers are only lowered by ten percent."

All of the Clients agreed, except Client One.

"How can we get the deaths back up?" asked Client One.

"There are several things we can do," said Spector who was a little annoyed. "I will do my best but at twenty-five thousand initially, the job will be done."

"Agreed then," said Client One.

"Thank you gentlemen," said Trott. "We will speak again after the event."

"*All Clients have left the conference,*" said the computer.

Spector sighed. He walked to a bar that was nestled in a corner and poured himself a drink. He would invite his security chief back in after he finished relaxing for a second.

"*Client six, contacting,*" said the computer suddenly.

"What?!" said Spector out loud putting down his drink. "Let it through."

A single panel of the monitor lit up showing Rylon Trott's unobscured face.

"Good evening, motherfucker," said Trott.

Spector was silent as he looked at the screen with disbelief. "You got balls," said Spector. "I will say that, kid."

"Don't mind trying to trace this," said Trott. "You won't be able to. I am long gone."

"I'll catch up with you soon," said Spector. "You had to know I'd figure it out. Your father is turning in his grave."

"Fuck him," said Trott, "and you, too."

"Why did you do it?" asked Spector taking his drink back.

"You know why. This shit is crazy and destructive. It won't work."

"Oh, yes it will," said Spector. "And when it does, I will personally oversee your public execution."

"Who was that woman who tried to kill me?" asked Trott. "Girlfriend?"

"At one point," said Spector. "You know me. She's very resourceful. You'll be seeing her soon. So, how did you escape. I'm curious."

"That bitch got hit by some running people after she blew up whatever it was outside," said Trott. "She shot a very lovely woman I was hoping to have sex with."

"Wherever you are, we will find you," said Spector. "You know that, don't you?"

"Not if I get you first," said Trott.

"How in the hell are you going to do that?" Spector laughed and took a gulp of his drink.

"I'm doing it now," said Trott. "Why do you think I would call? To keep you in that room. All I needed was a way to keep you from calling your people at the exact time— which is now."

Spector's mouth was agape as he heard an explosion and the sound of gunfire.

20

Freedom

The compression bombs exploded, knocking down the front door of Gregory Spector's home. The door blew and shards of wood and impaled the far wall. From the smoke and falling debris, Luther Green entered the home, the Baretta Storm out in front of him.

Luther looked up at the long spiral staircase in the foyer which was as spacious as any living room. He could hear men approaching.

"I'm in," said Luther into his comm radio.

"*No mercy,*" said Alex who was still outside, where five of Spector's security men lay dead, each of them having been shot in the head by Alex Deavers' silenced rifle.

Luther began to cut down the inside security men as they arrived and formed an assault flank on the second floor rising. He moved for cover in an adjacent room.

Low ground was not good and so he would have to move or they would outflank him soon.

"*Rear guards moving,*" said Alex in Luther's ear.

"Got it," said Luther.

Luther moved to his left, spraying his own cover fire. He pulled out a remote detonator and hit it. The power went out and the home was thrown into darkness.

"*We got about ten minutes to get him,*" said Alex. "*This place will be swarming with locals soon.*"

Luther put away his gun and pulled his battle knife. He switched to night vision and stalked the remaining guards.

He moved to the second floor from the rear. He saw two of them searching in the darkness. He waited until they came closer and then attacked, taking them both out in a manner of seconds.

Luther stepped passed the men, trying not to slip in the pool of spreading blood.

"*I'm inside,*" said Alex. "*Three bogeys to my right.*"

Luther heard three loud pops.

"*Neutralized,*" said Alex. "*No sign of Bane but I'll keep an eye out.*"

"That should be it," said Luther.

"*I'll keep any others at bay,*" said Alex.

Luther moved to the door leading to Spector's conference room and pulled the Storm. He moved to one side of the door and jiggled the door knob with the barrel of his gun.

There was a loud gunshot as a hole was blown into the door. Luther fired his weapon into the ceiling and another shot sounded, putting another hole in the door.

Luther got up from his crouch and opened the door from the other side through one of the holes.

Inside, he found Spector desperately trying to reload a shot gun.

"I can tell the sound of a double barrel," said Luther raising his gun. "Drop it."

Spector dropped the gun and the shells on the floor.

"Step away from it, carefully," said Luther.

Spector stepped away from the weapon.

"Mr. Green, I presume," said Spector who was backlit by a single computer terminal. "You here to take me in, or to rendition?"

"Arresting you was never an option," said Luther. "After I kill you, the others will panic and drop the plan."

"No, they won't," said Spector. "They will regroup and try again."

"We'll see," said Luther.

"You don't get it," said Spector. "The America you know is over one way or another. Listen, you can come out of this a wealthy man. You just erase Rylon Trott for us and Sharon Bane, too. She knows too much. I can guarantee you anything you want."

Luther was silent. He put the Storm down and raised the P99.

"You're bluffing! " said Spector. "You're not going to kill me. You want my information. I had insurance in case the plan went south. You can't get it if I'm dead."

"All the power in the house is out except this one bank of computers," said Luther. "It has a separate power source. That's where your information is located."

"You're wrong," said Spector nervously.

Everything Luther knew told him the man was lying. He could be wrong but he did not have a lot of time to find out. In this neighborhood, police response would be quick even though it would take some time to come to the remote location.

Luther did want to take Spector in and get all of the information he needed from him on video. This would go a long way to clear his name and any trouble he might be in.

"You need a live witness to corroborate," said Spector, clearly afraid now.

"I have Trott," said Luther.

"He'll disavow to save his ass," said Spector.

"I have him telling us everything on video, he doesn't know he was recorded. He was too scared because you had just tried to kill him."

Spector was silent. His mind searched for more reasons but none came to him.

"Name your price then," said Spector. "Name it."

Luther fired a shot into Spector's head. The tall man fell to the floor. Luther walked over and put another one into his heart.

"*Got company,*" said Alex still on the comm radio. "*Locals coming.*"

"Got it," said Luther.

Luther went to Spector's control panel. He lifted the top panel and cut the power in case it had a kill switch.

Luther removed the entire hard drive and rushed out of the house.

Luther and Alex met at the back of the place. They could hear sirens and see police cars approaching. They ran toward their SUV which was not far off.

"That it?" asked Alex.

"I hope so," said Luther. "If not, I'll be coming to Vegas to live with you."

"That would be fun," said Alex.

Suddenly, they were awash in light from a police helicopter. They were both taken by surprise because they did not hear it. In fact, they still heard little noise from it.

"Stealth copter," said Luther. "This ain't the police."

Alex raised his rifle but Luther stopped him.

"They could cut us down," said Luther. "It's the agency."

The copter lowered itself in their path, forcing them backwards as it landed. The blades slowed and the door opened.

Adelaide Gibson stepped out of the helicopter, wearing the company's standard navy suit. She still had her trademark grimace on her face and unamused pale blue eyes behind her glasses.

Two armed men jumped out in combat gear, guns raised.

"Stand down," said Adelaide, raising a hand. The men lowered their weapons.

She walked over to Luther and Alex, regarding the men. Luther was blood stained and holding the hard drive.

"Deavers," said Adelaide. "I knew you were too ornery to be dead."

"Adelaide," said Alex. "You're looking very old."

"I am old," said Adelaide without any trace of humor. "The incident at Patina was bad enough but two assaults in one night on billionaires, well, that had Luther Green written all over it."

"We need to leave, now," said Luther.

"Why would I want to do that?" asked Adelaide. "And by that I mean, why not take you and your pal here in?"

"Because Alex and I will kill those men and take that helicopter if you don't. Or, you'll have to kill us," said Luther.

A very uncomfortable moment passed. Adelaide was a friend but she did have her pride. Luther had threatened the head of the CIA and that was not a wise thing for anyone to do who had just committed multiple crimes.

"If it was anyone else," said Adelaide. "I wouldn't believe it. Your plan include shooting me?"

"And for that I would feel bad," said Luther, "but my mission is that important."

Adelaide regarded him for just a moment, then: "You clean on this?"

"Yes," said Luther. "I'll come in in a couple of days."

"Where's Sharon Bane?" asked Adelaide.

"I don't know," said Luther. "I thought I killed her but somehow she survived. She's turned and into this up to her eyeballs."

"You assume I know what *this* is," said Adelaide.

"Worse than what Kilmer did," said Luther.

Adelaide just stared at the two men again, the helicopter's engine made noises as it cooled down. She was tough enough to try them but knew their capabilities.

"Two days," said Adelaide. "Then I come looking for you myself." Into her comm radio she said: "Back perimeter all clear. Repeat, back clear."

Adelaide turned on her heel and got into the helicopter. It lifted off.

Alex and Luther sprinted off again.

"She trusts you," said Alex. "If it were just me, I'd be dead."

"She's a good woman," said Luther. "And she knows I'm not dirty."

They got to their vehicle and jumped in. Alex drove away as Luther inspected the hard drive component, hoping it contained Spector's insurance plan.

21

Trans

Suriname, Brasil

Sharon Bane looked out on the river from the Overbridge Resort in South America. She took another pain pill as she felt the tingling rise in her face under the bandages.

The procedure had taken over 20 hours and two days but these guys were the best facial recon doctors in the business.

She had seen herself before they wrapped her and it was awful but when she healed, no one would ever recognize her again. The doctor even fixed that sagging problem by tightening her muscle groups after he broke her jaw and reset it.

They changed her eyes from blue to light brown and gave her a new nose. The most amazing thing they did, however was they darkened her skin. All she had to do was keep taking the compound they gave her and she would look multiethnic forever.

Bane had been wise to run when Spector sent her back out to search for Rylon Trott. She had called in her funds, paid the fees and executed her escape plan.

It wasn't until she read about the siege on Spector's house, that she realized that Luther had been right under her nose. He was tracking her boss and when he realized that he had no way to stop him, he did what any good E-1 man would do, he moved to kill everyone.

Luther would never know why she was turned. Even Spector didn't know that she had gotten pregnant last year and terminated it.

She was not guilt-ridden or anything like that but she was painfully aware that she was a woman and her choices were soon to be limited.

The world was becoming a very small place and soon she would get old and then what? Marry some rich coot and watch as she withered? Pour herself into her work and maybe get killed? Or tie herself to a desk and dry up like Adelaide Gibson. No thanks.

No man would understand her choice. Too busy being men and having everything their way. It was a sweet deal she was offered and it would have solved all of her problems. The super rich ran the world no matter what men like Luther Green thought. Better throw in with them on the ground floor, than be a slave when they won.

But all of that was gone now because one man could not see his silly devotion to a theory that no longer meant anything. Soon, there would be only one government in the world and men like Luther Green would be in museums.

Luther had to know by now that she wasn't dead. If the agency had not reported her found, then Spector would have given her up before they killed him. He was a smart man but he would not be able to negotiate with Luther Green.

She could just go and forget about him. That would be the smart thing to do, she thought. But she could not shake the pain of being outsmarted and then there was the whole killing her thing. Something like that made a girl just a little angry.

If she went back to the U.S. to get him, she'd have to get through customs and whatever new high tech identification methods they were using. And even if she did, she still had to put him down, which was more than a notion.

She would heal, test drive her new body for a while, have some fun, sleep with some swarthy men and think about it.

There was a knock at her door.

"Betreden," said Bane in Dutch.

The nurse from the transition hospital came in. She had her little black bag of drugs and the big gun Bane knew she was carrying. Working for doctors who changed faces was dangerous work.

"I came to check on you, Miss 508," said the Nurse in Dutch. They only knew the numbers of the patients.

"I need more meds," said Bane.

"Very good," said the Nurse and gave Bane a new supply of pain killers.

"The doctors will be here in the morning to bandage you and take samples."

"Fine," said Bane.

"Very good Miss—"

"You can use my name," said Bane.

"Oh, no. It is not allowed."

"It's Okay. It's my new name. Call me Raven."

22

I.P.A.X.

Kingsport, Tennessee.

Luther and Alex did not dare go back to their safehouse. After all the commotion, it could not be trusted. They were holed up on the outskirts of Kentucky, in a rambling house close to the three-state border of Kentucky, and the Virginias. Both men were suspicious of their government and wanted to take no chances.

The house was spare and probably used as a vacation spot. But it was near a main interstate communication line, which had been easy to tap into from the relay point.

Spector's hard drive was encrypted and it had taken the better part of a day to get around it. What they found was about two decades of information, detailed conversations, video and classified documentation that no civilian should have. It also contained the full plan to alter the U.S.

The weapons system that was going to be used had been developed in the 1950's as part of the first laser program started from an obscure paper by Albert Einstein.

The Inverse Particle Algorithmic Expression was a theory by which matter could be accelerated and disbursed into smaller parts with some turning into energy. In short, a disintegration beam.

Early attempts failed and several scientists were killed or injured in these tests. The project was scrapped in 1972, but of course, it just went underground.

The computer age and several new theories and processors had probably made it finally work, only now it was in the hands of non-governmental powers.

The shooting at Patina and Spector's home were being called acts of domestic terrorism and several hate groups were being conveniently targeted.

Unofficially, the FBI and CIA were looking for Sharon Bane who was probably out of the country by now if she was smart.

Luther did not like this last fact because it meant he'd be looking over his shoulder for the near future.

"You're going to have to find her and kill her, you know," said Alex. "She's figured it out by now."

"I know," said Luther.

Luther made a copy of everything Spector had and sent it to his online lock box. Then he made another copy and gave it to Alex. Now, both of them were protected if anything went wrong.

"This has been a wild ride," said Alex. "I look forward to going back home and being a ghost."

"You don't want to come to D.C. with me?" said Luther. "Pretty sure the President is going to attend."

"I'll pass," said Alex.

Luther drove Alex to the train station. Deavers was still afraid to fly as he was probably still on the no fly list. Adelaide had seemed like she didn't care that he was still among the living but he wasn't counting on her forgiveness.

The two friends said goodbye with a hug and no words. Neither man was given to emotion in these moments but they exposed as much as they could.

Luther watched Alex walk off towards the train, knowing that he was the only person in the world that he fully trusted, a man whom he had tried to kill not long ago.

Luther returned to the new safehouse and put on his dress uniform. When he met with officials, he was still officially an Army Captain.

Luther regarded himself in the mirror. He'd never gotten to serve really and wondered what it might have been like in a platoon, combat action and lifelong friendships, instead of the very lonely life of an assassin.

Suddenly, he heard his perimeter warning sound. He'd set up a crude but effective system in case anyone wandered by. As he registered the noise, he immediately moved to action, understanding that this mission was not quite over.

Luther grabbed his sidearm and moved toward the front of the house. It could be Alex returning but he did not think so. Bane was the first name that entered his head or perhaps one of the Core members was trying to tie up loose ends or seek revenge.

Luther moved slowly toward the front of the place as he heard someone jimmy the door. And then heavy footsteps as two men entered and then... women's shoes?

"I know you're here, Green," said Adelaide Gibson. "And I know you hear us coming, so come on out."

Adelaide stood in the living room as Luther stepped into the area. She stood in her sensible suit flanked by the same two guards he'd seen outside of Spector's home. They were both armed but their weapons were pointed down. Adelaide held a .45 by her waist.

Luther lowered his weapon. He quickly went over all of his moves and wondered how she had found him.

Adelaide had once broken into his D.C. place and left a warning and so she did have skills. He was impressed and unnerved at the same time.

"My two days aren't up yet," said Luther.

"That's why I gave you two, so I could find you," said Adelaide. "So, where is it?"

"There," said Luther pointing to Spector's hard drive.

"Good," said Adelaide. She instructed the guards to take the hard drive, which they did. They also took the rest of Luther's computer equipment and exited.

"I know you made a copy," said Adelaide, "but I wouldn't count on it being online. We found your little backdoor and closed it."

"I haven't been shot," said Luther, "so I suppose all's forgiven." He put his sidearm away.

"No," said Adelaide. "We can't have you do what you did to the last President. This information is too crucial."

"Don't suppose you want to tell me how you found me," said Luther.

"I don't suppose I do," said Adelaide. "Let's just say I'm older than you."

"How could we let some assholes come this close to creating this kind of chaos?" Luther was looking for answers if she had any.

"I just work here," said Adelaide. "again that comes under the heading of age."

"And what about the men who tried to take over your country?" said Luther. "You mad about that at all."

"Yes but they're going to buy their way out of it," said Adelaide.

"Tell me you did not say the word *buy*," said Luther.

"What country do you think you live in, Green? For a man who loves America, you don't seem to understand it very well."

Silence fell between the two friends and Luther noticed for the first time that Adelaide was still armed.

"I put my gun away some time ago," said Luther. "You're still holding yours."

"Didn't bring my purse," said Adelaide.

And then there was that moment that every agent dreads, that two or three seconds when you don't know whether or not the agent before you was sent to retrieve you or eliminate you.

Adelaide was benign in appearance but had her share of kills in the field and now as a company woman, she would certainly carry out the order.

"Come on," said Adelaide. "They're all waiting for you back in D.C."

****

Washington, D.C.

Luther was helicoptered into D.C. and was soon in another room with one high level member of the DOD, Homeland, the FBI and the man who had no designation, the Spook.

In the middle of the party, was the Vice President who did not look happy to be there. The President, obviously wanted no part of something this tainted. This was dangerous, high level shit work.

"Captain Green," said the Vice President. "These allegations are very serious and a lot of damage has been done. I'm getting disturbing calls from some powerful men."

"Everything in my report is true," said Luther. "I think you all know that. What we should be concerned with is how we can stop this from happening again."

"We can't," said the main from the DOD. This sentiment was echoed by several others.

"We live in a democracy," said the Vice President. "A capitalist democracy where certain talented or fortunate men and women will always have great wealth and great ambition."

"Then we need to place safeguards," said Luther.

"We have our Constitution," said the man from the FBI.

"And we have you," said the Spook and he laughed but it was not derisive. It was dark humor. Men like Luther were the final solution.

"I understand we're negotiating with the men who composed The Core," said Luther. "I propose that we don't."

"And what should we do?" asked the man from Homeland.

"Kill them," said Luther. "Discourage others."

"One was enough," said the man from the DOD. "I think people will get the message."

"Fellas," said the Vice President. "I do not want to hear this. Captain Green, you are being promoted to Lieutenant effective immediately."

"Thank you, sir," said Luther.

"That's it for me," said the Vice-President. "This is all I am allowed to hear. Congratulations, Lieutenant."

The Vice -President left with his compliment. Then the DOD and FBI leaders left, leaving Luther alone with just the Spook.

"We're starting E-1 again," said one of them. "That's why we wanted to see you. We've already chosen a new director."

"I'd be happy to work with Adelaide," said Luther. He could not hide his happiness at this news.

"Not her," said the Spook. "She's retiring. We got a new man in mind."

For a moment, Luther thought he was going to be offered the job, the Spook hit the intercom and asked for the man to be sent in.

Luther almost fell from his chair when Alex Deavers walked in. He was dressed in company attire and he did not look happy.

"Missed my train," said Alex.

"Mr. Deavers will run the new E-1 and you will train the new recruits," said the spook. "The Agency will oversee." The last word was pronounced with a touch of sarcasm.

"Look," said Alex, "I agreed to this because it's preferable to being shot but Luther is not going to be some teacher. I need him in the field. I've been briefed and we need him out there— right now."

"We're good with that," said the Spook. "That's it, fellas. Pay raises and good wishes all around. Welcome back."

Luther and Alex walked out of the room and down the long hallway. If this was all real, then they'd just saunter out and begin their work. If not, there would be a black van at the door with armed men and this was the end.

"That pain you feel is getting fucked without lubrication," said Alex.

"Did they get your copy of the Core's information?" asked Luther.

"Yes," said Alex. "Motherfuckers were waiting for me when I got on. Stopped the train a mile out and raided it. What about you?"

"They got the drive and my copy. Adelaide found me."

"Man, she is good."

The two men walked out of the building. There was no black van and kill team waiting, just the day and a lovely blue sky.

They stopped at the top of the stairs and looked out on the capitol. As always, it was beautiful.

"I don't get this," said Alex. "Why are we not dead?"

"They need us," said Luther. "They know we have to protect our freedom and only men like us can do it. In the end, we're patriots and that still counts." Luther smiled a little.

"Fuck me," said Alex laughing. "You had another copy."

"They burned by online locker and closed my backdoor but it triggered an automatic remote back up. I'm sure the hacker saw the code. They know, but we're all acting like I didn't cover my ass."

"Then I don't have to work for these fucks," said Alex.

"I'd appreciate it if you wouldn't quit before we can get E-1 back," said Luther.

"I am intrigued by that," said Alex. "And I like giving orders."

"Then let's do it," said Luther. "Let's start some trouble."

The two men walked off into the capitol. Luther did so with more than a little hope that his words about patriotism were still true.

Made in the USA
San Bernardino, CA
22 July 2017